THE Lost Treasure OF THE DARIÉN GAP

THE MOST DANGEROUS JUNGLE IN THE WORLD!

BOOK IV OF *THE LOST EL DORADO* SERIES

W. MICHAEL GAZDAR, DC

© 2022. All rights reserved.

W. MICHAEL GAZDAR, D.C.
Walnut Creek, California

Published and distributed by: John Muir Chiropractic Center (JMCC)
First Edition: 2022

2021 Ygnacio Valley Road, Suite C-204
Walnut Creek, California 94598
Phone: (925) 939-2225
Fax: (925) 939-8017
Email: michael@gazdar.com
Web: www.michaelgazdar.com

This book is a work of fiction. Names, characters, places and incidents are products of the author's imagination, and are used factitiously. Any resemblance to actual events, local people or persons living or dead is entirely coincidental.
No part of this book may be reproduced without the author's written permission.

Library of Congress Catalogue Number: 2021924659
Gazdar, Michael

THE LOST TREASURE OF THE DARIÉN GAP - THE MOST DANGEROUS JUNGLE IN THE WORLD

ISBN (e book): 978-0-9645301-8-8

ISBN (Trade Paperback): 978-0-9645301-7-1

Printed in the United States of America

ACKNOWLEDGEMENTS

Thank you to the following people who have helped make this book
a reality:

Cover Design by: Emily's World of Design

Publishing Assistance: Eric Van Der Hope

Back Cover Photo by: CBJ Gazdar

Formatting by: Nicole Hayley Art

Beta Readers: Janet Baillie
Captain Paul Ruff
Marilyn Hubbard

DEDICATION

This book is dedicated to my wife, Teri and our three sons, Christian,
Brandon and Jonathan.

You guys are my family, my loves and my life. Thank you.

CONTENTS

PROLOGUE

THE DARIÉN GAP 1946

THIS JUNGLE WAS DANGEROUS, THOUGHT JAKE Marley, *damn dangerous,* as his flat-bottomed skiff rolled across the Atrato River in the middle of the Darién Gap. His guide, Diego, and armed bodyguards Antonio and Maltilda kept him moving deep into the jungle toward the hidden gold mines, near Cana. He was unarmed, except for his large steel machete and his eight-inch Bowie knife, but his crew all carried old fashioned M-1 rifles, side-arm hand guns and their own machete knives. When they had neared the abandoned gold mines, Jake listened as Diego and Antonio, said in dark whispers, that they were now in the eye in the jungle, and had been identified. Their lives were in forfeit for bringing this white man down to the sacred shores with them. Only Maltilda, was fearless and remained faithful, as he steadily guided the 35-horsepower motor sending them upstream. He was a local native who never gave in to the local superstitions and was only motivated by money, which would help his family, back down river.

Jake was from Queensland, Australia, and, like Maltilda, not a superstitious sort. He was a practical man, standing six feet, two inches tall and weighing in at 235 pounds. He played rugby for the National title and was only dispatched because of a knee injury. Other than that, he was always ready to do battle with anyone and everyone who crossed him or got in his way. He took on any and all comers and his fights in the Australian pubs were legendary.

As the skiff was about to touch shore, Maltilda cut the engines, allowing it to slip into the shore and gently come to rest. It was eerily quiet as they stepped out of the boat and Jake, checking his maps, gazed into the jungle. The map indicated the mines were a short distance up ahead.

He studied the mountain pass, to the left of him and the jungle before him. He knew moving ahead could mean death, but he had to trust there was still gold in these mines and that he could find it. He thought back to the Australian rugby tournament where he met a grizzled old spectator, who had been rambling to his friends about the lost gold in the Darién Gap, and how he needed to get back down there. In Jake, he found a friendly ear, as Jake was fascinated by lost gold and the possibility of striking it rich. This is what had brought him on this quest after over a year of planning it out. Now, he wasn't so sure.

Jake took a minute to study the old map, which he had found in an Australian antique store, inside an old book, from 1908, about a gold strike in the jungle of the Darién Gap. It intrigued him, and with renewed focus, he made his way forward, followed by the two bodyguards, Antonio and Maltilda. Having fulfilled his agreement to get Jake to the spot on the Atrato River closest to the gold mines, Diego stayed back to protect the boat.

They had traveled into the jungle for about one quarter of a kilometer, when Jake saw what was clearly an abandoned ore carrying trolly. It lay on its side next to a torn up severely rusted track ravaged by the damp jungle air. Jake hoped he could follow the track back to the gold mine, but it had already been stripped away, likely due to the value of the steel.

The three of them moved through the jungle carefully. It was just after the war, and they had no idea what they might find here in this jungle between Panama and Colombia. The air was humid, the jungle was wet. Jake was following a thin line on the map that led to a mountain, but then stopped. There was no "X" that marked the gold, but on the flip side of the map, were some hand drawings of what looked like a chamber, inside a rock formation, and the words *oro macizo/puro*, (solid, pure gold). This made no sense, because the gold, if there was any, should be in ore form, not pure, refined gold. This intrigued him from the moment he first saw the map back in Australia.

As they walked closer to the mountains, the jungle became denser and very ominous. Maltilda took the lead and, using his machete, began cutting a path through the foliage in front of them. Suddenly a giant anaconda, at least twenty feet long, slithered out of the trees and fell on Antonio, who was at the rear! Draped around his shoulders, the weight of the giant anaconda knocked him to the ground. The head, as big as a small dog hissed menacingly at Jake, who had turned to help. The snake began to coil around Antonio as he screamed for help! Maltilda carefully swung his machete, enough to cut into the snake's body and thwart its attack, while sparing Antonio any harm. Antonio threw the snake's body off his shoulders and scooted backwards, still seated, with his hands and arms. Rather than pursue and kill the injured anaconda, Maltilda, let it slither into the dense jungle.

Jake moved back toward Antonio and helped him to his feet. The terrified bodyguard muttered and yelled in his native language, while covering his ears with his hands, was shaking madly. Jake pulled out a flask of brandy and made him drink it. The fiery liquid burned deep into his throat, but the heat spread through his body and calmed him down. They continued moving forward after Antonio thanked Maltilda profusely, sweat pouring off his brow, as they moved ahead.

They made it to the base of the mountain, which towered over them by over one thousand meters. As they walked around, they could hear what sounded like splashing water. After about one hundred meters, they came to a small lagoon, with a waterfall, cascading down from the side of the mountain. It was not a big waterfall, but enough to fill the lagoon with water and feed a stream that disappeared into the jungle.

Jake checked the map, but the line had ended at the mountain. He flipped it over and looked at the hand drawing. The chamber was somewhere inside this mountain, but there was no visible opening and no way to get inside. The left side of the map showed the side of the mountain with the chamber to the right. He was baffled. He held the map up to the sunlight, which was forcing its way through the dense jungle. His eyes squinted.

Suddenly, he saw something on the far-right side of the map, which looked like a waterfall. Vertical lines fell from the top of the map to the bottom, then ran horizontally off the map. There was a small circle drawn at the bottom. *Could that represent the lagoon and the waterfalls,* he wondered. He looked at the jagged edges of both sides of the map. He took the map and slowly, gently began to separate it down the middle. It was easily done, as it looked like it had been separated before and he was now holding two halves of the map. He took the right edge, with the vertical lines and placed it next to the left side which showed the mountain and the chamber beyond. The torn edges lined up perfectly and he knew the map had been deliberately separated. It had never occurred to him why one side of the map showed the way to the mine and the other was just a rambling jungle. It was because the map had been cut in half. The new arrangement made much more sense.

He studied the lines, which were the waterfall and the lagoon on the left side, the wall of the mountain to the right and the chamber to the right of it. It became clear what he needed to do. Jake turned to Maltilda and Antonio. "I need to go for a swim and I need one of you to come with me."

Maltilda and Antonio looked at each other. Antonio was still taking small swigs off the flask of brandy, and did not seem inclined to have any more adventures that day. He quietly shook his head no. Maltilda, the braver of the two, looked at the lagoon. It was relatively clear and there were no signs of piranha or anything else that looked dangerous.

"Amigo," Maltilda said good-naturedly, "Why are we going for a swim? Are you hot?"

Jake smiled, but didn't laugh. He was serious about his quest and realized the chamber and, hopefully the gold, was somewhere on the other side of this lagoon. "No, but I need to see what is on the other side of this waterfall, and I think it might be what we are looking for."

"I'll go," said Maltilda. "I can swim good! I'll haul your ass out if you drown!"

"I'm a rugger, Maltilda! I play the toughest game in the world, and I can swim faster than anyone on my rugby team. You just follow my lead under there and be ready to come back if we start to run out of air."

Maltilda nodded. Jake put the map back into the waterproof bag it had been in, and then, took a swig of water from his canteen. Maltilda also drank some water out of his own canteen. Antonio, took another drink from the flask of brandy.

"Don't get drunk, Antonio," Jake said, "We'll need you when we bring out the stacks of gold!" Antonio nodded, placing the flask on the ground in front of the rock he was sitting on and plugged the cork into the bottle. He picked up his rifle and got to his feet, looking around at the jungle, which seemed to lean in on them as they stood by the lagoon.

Maitilda was holding his M-1 rifle and decided it would be safe to swim with it for a little while under the water, because he might need it on the other side of the mountain. Both men stayed in their clothes and boots. Jake entered the water first, looking down. It was mostly rocky on the bottom, with some sand and silt. He began to plane out and move across the surface of the lagoon toward the waterfall. Maltilda entered the water and followed him. Suddenly, Jake jackknifed and disappeared under the water. Maltilda waited until he was at the same spot and followed him down.

Jake pulled himself forward until he was under the water fall, which hit him hard on his back as he proceeded to move beyond the waterfall. He felt along the rocks at the bottom and pulled himself against them. Ahead of him, he could see light and, feeling himself running out of air, made a mighty dash forward and surfaced into the light. He looked around and realized he was in a small chamber. The light was from a natural shaft extending to the top of the mountain, which also let in air. It was musty, but it was better than nothing. Maltilda surfaced behind him and looked around. They were able to climb onto a rock ledge and lay there for a minute panting.

Jake got up and felt along the rocky walls. They were porous like volcanic lava flow that had hardened over the centuries. *Was this it?* thought Jake, *This one small ante room, barely four meters across?* He looked across the pool of water, they had emerged from. The ledge extended around, and he could see what looked like a small opening on the other side. By then, Maltilda had gotten out of the water, carrying his rifle, and they walked together over to the other side. The opening was merely a slit in the rocks, but it was wide enough for the men to slip through. Jake pulled out a torchlight, he had purchased in London just after the war, out of his waterproof bag. They walked down a dark narrow passage, dimly lit by the torchlight. They walked a few meters until they rounded a bend. Suddenly it was lighter, as the chamber opened up, and, like the first room they had been in, was also illuminated by an opening to the sky. This chamber was much larger and looked like it was over three hundred meters across. Mostly circular, but with ragged edges, it looked to be more promising than the small chamber they had just left.

As he swept his torchlight around, he suddenly saw a faint glint of metal on the other side of the room. "Maltilda!" he hissed, "Look over there!"

Miltada nodded, *"Sí, mi amigo,* but let's be careful! Don't touch anything!"

Jake nodded and moved toward the metal. Once there, they realized there were solid gold bars, each weighing a kilogram or more, stacked on top of each other. There were hundreds of them.

"Mi Dios mio!" said Maltilda.

Jake reached in and took out one of the bars. He held it up to the light. That's when all hell broke loose.

The walls started shaking and the chamber began to collapse on itself. The shifting of the rocks, cut out the light from above and they were left in the darkness. Suddenly, as Jake and Matilda turned around, they were attacked by beings, seemingly, not of this earth. They both screamed as they were attacked and cut down. Both men fought furiously against what, they did not know. Suddenly Jake felt his lungs implode as something sharp was thrust into his chest. He screamed and yelled for Maltilda to take the gold bar, as he knew his wound was mortal. "Get out of here!" he hissed.

Maltilda did not want to leave his *padrone,* but he knew he had to get away. His legs and arms had been cut by something, but he didn't know what. He felt the loss of blood, but was able to grab the gold brick from Jake and sprinted for the small chamber. He reached it and dove head-first into the water, dropping his rifle behind him. By dead reckoning, he reached the surface of the lagoon. He propelled himself out of the water and started to call for Antonio. Suddenly, by the light of the fading afternoon, he saw Antonio. His throat had been cut and he was lying on his back, with his eyes wide open staring at the overhead trees.

Maltilda, still holding the gold bar ran to the trail, leading him back to the beach. He heard things behind him, screaming to get to him, but he was too adept and would make it outside, no matter what!

He reached the skiff, but there was no sign of Diego. Holding the brick, he jumped inside and fired up the engine. Suddenly he saw Diego. His body had been tied upside down to a branch in a huge tree, over twelve feet off the ground. His arms were dangling straight down as if imploring him to stop. His eyes were wide open, as was his mouth, but no scream would ever again escape from his throat. It was obvious he was dead. Maltilda gunned the engines and shot down the river, never to return again.

CHAPTER ONE

THE PANAMANIANS AND THE AMERICANS

THE CUBAN GENERAL WAS SEATED IN THE command chair of his brown water boat. They were moving up the water on the Atrato River in the Darién Gap, the most dangerous jungle in the world. His name was General Xavier De Luna and he was in command of this region of the jungle. His crew moved slaves, money, cocaine and other "products" across the river between Panama and Columbia. Heavily financed by Communist insurgents, they were at war with many other nefarious factions on the river.

The main battle was between his group, the *Fuerzas Armandas Revolucionarias Armed Forces de Panama y Columbia, (FARP),* (The Revolutionary Forces of Panama and Colombia) against the Columbian Government. FARP controlled the Atrato River and used it and the surrounding jungle land to move between Panama and Colombia. They were at war with the legitimate governments of both countries and employed a system of bribes to top officials that allowed them to ply their trade on both ends of the river with minimal interference. Unfortunately, the Columbian and Panamanian officials changed every time there was shakeup in the government. When the demands changed, depending on the whims of the controlling power, several guerrilla groups would spring up and fight each other, each with its own agenda.

Getting in the way, were the independent smugglers, drug runners, slave traders and immigrants trying to get to the United States from South America, through Panama, Costa Rica, Nicaragua, Honduras, Guatemala and Mexico. Added to the mix were gold seekers, searching for the vast wealth of the Lost Treasure of the Darién Gap, which was rumored to be in a mine near the Atrato River. Some of the old ones spoke of the cache, inside an extinct volcano, exceeding one hundred million U.S. dollars in gold bars and bullion.

General De Luna looked out at the brown water and the high cliffs, which surrounded the Atrato River. They were meeting a boat of smuggles carrying six kidnapped women, who were from the United States and Mexico, intended for sale. They had been sent to supply his chain, which led up to the very top of his organization – millionaires and billionaires who purchased women from all parts of the globe, but especially the United States. The women from there were beautiful and, as was pleasing to their intended masters, could be strong-willed and demanding. According to these customers, they were spoiled and needed to be dominated and punished for their attitudes. They were sold with the intention of breaking their spirit and forcing them into submission. Thus, their new masters would be dubbed *"Men of Men,"* who, like the sultans of old, kept stables of women to pleasure them and, if they were not pleased, were simply dumped in the desert, dead or alive.

Normally, a man like General De Luna would be considered of too high a rank to do such mundane tasks, such as picking up new slaves, or meeting a boat full of cocaine, but he enjoyed the challenge. At the age of 45, he was a relatively young General and only had to answer directly to the commanders in Cartagena and a local Supreme General, who was actually even younger than him. Because he came from Cuba, he was tied in to the Communist Party Machine, which extended all the way back to China and North Korea. Much smaller than the party was when Russia was the former Soviet Union, the factions were still strong and the local fighters, ferocious. General De Luna suspected some of the work they did, which was obviously illegal, still served a purpose by helping fund their fight against the Nationals, and also those small-time smugglers, who were out for their own gain.

General De Luna's boat was a sixty-foot command boat, with machine guns, rocket launchers, and the ability to get away from danger very quickly. Based on a British model of a modern rescue boat, it was primed with a shallow draft and deadly munitions.

His first officer, at the helm announced, "We are almost at the rendezvous spot, General. Should we stop, or keep going forward, sir?"

General De Luna, looking through his binoculars, scanned the cliffs and then down the river. He saw no hostilities. Suddenly a small skiff appeared down river and proceeded toward his boat. Approximately thirty feet long, it moved forward at thirty knots. The General could see at least six girls on the deck, along with several soldiers guarding them. They were approaching fast and he told his deck officer to come about and halt the boat.

His craft turned to port and stopped, exposing its starboard side of his vessel, rocking in its own violent wake. "Bring your weapons to the starboard!" he yelled out to his men. Several moved forward and laid on their stomachs holding their AK-47s aimed at the soldiers on the skiff.

The approaching boat began to slow, seeing the intent of the General's boat. They pulled up and made a hard stop in the river, fifty yards away from each other. The smugglers also brandished their weapons and made it very clear, they were prepared to fire. It appeared they wanted something more than the agreed upon terms. In any event, it was too late to renegotiate.

It was a standoff. The General pulled out a megaphone. In Spanish, he said, "Secure your weapons! We will come alongside and collect the girls. We have the agreed funds. We will wait for you to respond." He paused, "Or we will blow you out of the water, now!"

The General could see the girls being moved behind a shield and the mercenaries moving up to the front with machine guns and stinger missiles. Someone answered in Spanish, "These are prime women! The price is now double!"

"Gentlemen!" General De Luna yelled into his megaphone, "This does not have to end in bloodshed! We have the agreed funds. We have the agreements in place with your military. We also have the strength to take what we want. If you fire on us or harm the women, we will be forced to attack and we will not stop until you are all dead! So please think about that BEFORE you act!" he screamed into the megaphone.

Suddenly, the soldiers on the skiff opened fire on the General's boat.

"Pull back!" yelled the General. "Commence firing!"

They opened up, as the screaming girls fell back into the stern of the boat behind the Kevlar shields.

Both sides took casualties. The firing stopped suddenly as the all of the smugglers died or were seriously wounded during the cross fire. The girls were still screaming hysterically; surrounded by dead soldiers. De Luna's boat turned and moved ahead slowly, as his men aimed their AK-47's at the skiff, ready to execute any remaining mercenaries, who might be a problem. As they moved to the side of the boat, they could see the dead soldiers and the women in the stern. They were no longer screaming, but were clearly terrified.

The General's boat pulled up alongside the skiff and his men jumped onboard to transfer the women, who began to climb onboard the boat. The General stood as they came onboard. He said in both Spanish and English, "Ladies, you are our prisoners. We will not harm you as long as you cooperate with us. We promise you safe passage to Cartagena, where you may contact your families to make the customary ransom requests, which will not be unreasonably denied. My promise to you, is that none of my soldiers will molest you and you will be safe to relax on our boat." He smiled and spread his arms out, as if to show he was speaking the truth in earnest.

This was a lie, of course. The women had already been sold into slavery, but the less they knew about their intended fate, the less trouble they would be.

With little fanfare, the girls were all escorted below deck

and given water, wine and some good native food, for which they were grateful. They began to relax, which was all part of the plan. It was the first time they had been treated with kindness since being snatched off their streets of their cities. Several traded stories of how they would be rescued by their families, who they were sure had been notified.

As the boat moved out, General De Luna looked back at the bullet-riddled skiff he had defeated and, once they were out of range, watched as it was detonated by his crew. The boat was ignited with a huge explosion and the soldiers' bodies were lost forever. The General smiled. He was going to honor his agreement, but since they had not, he had another sixty thousand dollars he could keep and still collect the money for the women. He stared at the wake of his vessel as they pulled away and got up to speed. *Life was good,* he thought.

****

Jazmine Paris had a secret life that no one knew about. She wanted to be a famous actress in Hollywood, but she told her friends she just wanted to sing, dance and act locally-just for fun. Barely 5'0", she had just turned 18 and weighed 100 pounds. Unbeknownst to her family, she had a huge crush on the offensive tackle of her high school team. All her friends were attracted to the team quarterback, a hot-shot wide receiver, and the fast linebackers; but she loved Steph Hayward, the Offensive Tackle for San Ramon Valley High School. He was big, 255 pounds, tall, over 6'4", sometimes obnoxious, but with a sweet side. He could easily transition from throwing hundreds of Fizzies into the high school pool as a joke, to stopping his teammates from intimidating the new wimpy kid who had just moved here from Los Angeles. Then, like now, when he brought Jazmine candy and flowers because she didn't get cast as the lead in the school play, *West Side Story.* Steph was a good person and cared about people, especially Jazmine.

He sat outside the auditorium during the audition, and could tell by her face, that she had lost out on the lead role. As a consolation, she was offered a lesser part as one of the gang girls. She sat down next to him with a brave face and said she would probably take the part offered to her. Then she broke down and cried into his big arms, as he held her.

He never said a word, letting her cry it out. Finally, through sniffles, she said, "Am I being a baby?" She looked up into his eyes.

Steph smiled at her. "No," he said, "The lead is going to Cindy."

Jazmine pushed away and looked at him. "How the hell do you know that?" she asked sharply. "The Cast List hasn't even been published yet!"

"They hired a professional director from Hollywood, because the production was going down the tubes and they want to make money on it. His niece is our classmate, Cindy. It's not what you know, or how good you are. It is who you know." His voice trailed off. "Fuck 'em. Everyone knows you're the best and it will probably bomb. She's pretty, but not a very good actress. Play your part with gusto and everyone will see that you should have gotten the lead. Sometimes it's best to let everything play out, and then, when it is a total fuck up, they realize they screwed up! If I were you, I'd keep learning the lead part inside and out, and be ready when the play is about to implode!"

Jazmine lowered her head into his lap. "Thanks Steph," she said. "And thanks for the candy and the flowers. I don't always know how you know these things, but I am really glad you like me.

The 1:00 Bell rang and she jumped up. "I have to get to Professor Roberto's class," she exclaimed. "He has a big announcement about a trip to Panama, to teach kids English for ten days!"

Steph smiled, "I know you'll be asked because you speak Spanish better than anyone in the school!"

Jazmine smiled at him, "I hope so!" she squealed. "By the way, I love you!" she said and raced off to her class.

Steph smiled. He loved her too and he hoped she would be safe if she made it to Panama.

Once inside the class, Jazmine took her seat near the front of the class. *Señor Morales*, handed out flyers which would explain the trip to Panama to teach English to the locals from the villages of the jungles. He went over it with the whole class. It would cost $1,200.00, but that included all transportation, food, medical clearances and immunizations as needed. The tutors had to be in Spanish AP classes, with at least an A- average. They had to be healthy and allowed to travel internationally by their parents.

They would land in Colon and be transported to the school. They would be fed, protected and a citation would be sent to their colleges of choice, that they had done this voluntary service for a Third World Country.

There was a buzz in the classroom after he handed out the paperwork. Most of them were not at an A- level, but at least four of the girls qualified, including Jazmine.

He held up his hand. He was thirty-six years of age, in very good shape and, according to many of the girls, was quite handsome, with dark eyes, a wide mustache and big brown eyes. He resembled photos of *Poncho Villa* in his younger days. He looked around at all of the faces and smiled. "I know everyone wants to go on this trip, but only a few may go!" he said earnestly. "I will expect applications from those of you who wish to go, but may not have the financial means or quite the GPA to make the trip. We will consider all applicants!" He smiled. "Those who are interested may start the paperwork now and those of you who are not, may start working on Chapter Twelve in the workbook."

Roberto looked across the room at the kids who were working earnestly on the applications. He was excited about this trip, because he would be seeing some of his friends from his high school and college days. He had done this trip several times and his reputation for bringing down bright American students was growing and appreciated by the local Panamanian government.

****

Roberto was born into a good family, but a few events along the way had gotten him into trouble. He had his humble beginnings in Panama City, born to his mother, who taught English in the local school and his father, who had worked on, and helped maintain the Panama Canal. He was an only child, whose sister had died of fever at six months old. This had changed his mother, who, instead of holding her remaining child close, had grown emotionally distant from both him and his father.

His father had immersed himself in his work, and was seldom home. Thus, Roberto Morales had grown up virtually alone, seeking solace in the one thing he could control-books. He read everything he could get his hands on. Fortunately, his mother had a large collection of books in the house, and the local library was only two blocks away, near his school.

When Roberto had turned 12, he began to notice the girls in his grade, and they didn't look as sinister as they had when he was younger. In fact, some were quite pretty. He admired them from afar, being too shy to actually talk to them. Two years later, when he was in high school, one girl finally broke the ice and asked him to the Freshman dance, which he accepted happily, although somewhat awkwardly. Her name was Mary, and she came from a good, very religious Catholic family. They had had a wonderful time at the dance and they stayed together for the next three years.

The one drawback was, that Mary had a cousin, whom she loved and worried about, named Juan Velasco. Only three years her senior, he was already a degenerate gambler. Much to Mary's dismay, Juan liked Roberto immensely and took him under his wing to teach him all about the joys of gambling and ways to cheat the system. Juan cheated the local gambling houses, as well as people he met on the street, who were also cheaters themselves. Roberto didn't complain about Juan's antics and the seeds for his gambling addiction had been planted.

Finally, one day, after Mary begged Roberto to please stop seeing Juan, he relented and told Juan they had to part ways. By then, Roberto was a senior in high school and, because he was a soccer star on the school team and also on an elite travel team, Juan asked him for one last favor. Juan knew Roberto had been passed over for a scholarship at the local university, but still needed money to attend college. So, he asked him to help throw the championship game between Panama City and Oxford School. He didn't want him to be obvious about it, but just miss a few shots here and there, so that Oxford would win and Juan would collect a large sum of money, which he would split with Roberto. Against his better judgement, Roberto agreed.

During the game, which was a wild one, neither side could score. Roberto kept his promise to miss a few shots, none of which were easy, but ones he thought he could have made under normal circumstances. His teammates, were the ones who noted his lack of enthusiasm for the game and began to avoid kicking the ball to him, whenever possible.

During a final rest period, his coach approached Roberto, while he was panting on the sidelines. Coach Perez was a sharp coach and had played on the Panama national football team, the *Selección de fútbol de Panamá*. He could see his star player was not performing up to his usual game. He had a sense that something was amiss, but he didn't want to make any false accusations that Roberto was not really trying to win, so he came up with a better plan. Knowing Roberto had not gotten any offers for college, he had contacted a former national teammate of his, who was the head coach at the *Universidad de Panama*, and had told him about Roberto.

Quietly, he whispered into Roberto's ear, that his friend was in the stands and was going to offer him a full ride to the University, but was disappointed so far with Roberto's play. With less than a minute remaining in the game, and tied zero to zero, he encouraged Roberto to make a play and help them win the title. Roberto, still looking down at the ground, nodded and made a decision that would change his life forever.

The ball was tossed in and kicked back and forth by his teammates, who were avoiding Roberto. Suddenly, just as the clock reached the five second mark, Roberto, with his back to the goal and 20 feet away ran forward and intercepted a pass that was going across the field, meant for someone else. In a move that looked like Pelé, he snatched the ball with his right foot and, with a shot known as the bicycle kick, spun upside down, firing the ball past the shocked outstretched hands of the Oxford goalie, scoring just as time ended, and winning the game for Panama City. The stands erupted and Roberto, lying on his back looking skyward, knowing the shot had gone in, was mobbed by his teammates. The TV and radio announcers were screaming into their respective microphones, while the shot was replayed over and over on television.

For his part, Roberto, instead of jumping up and running around like most soccer players do after making a goal, not to mention, a spectacular title-winning shot, simply laid on the ground, crying his eyes out. His teammates thought they were tears of joy, but it was tears of fear, as now he had to face his girlfriend's cousin Juan, who, sitting in the stands looking on, was scarlet with rage.

Finally, his teammates pulled him of the ground and lifted him to their shoulders. Coach Perez and several students ran past the sideline guards, mobbing everyone on the team. After a wild celebration, the crowd calmed down, and the team made their way to the center of the field, where an awards stand had been brought out. The trophies and medals were given out and, to no one's surprise, Roberto was awarded the MVP of the game, in spite of his protests of having had a really bad game and didn't deserve it. But his protests fell on deaf ears, as the crowd chanted, *"Roberto, Roberto, Roberto,"* over and over again.

Finally, they retired to the locker room with everyone slapping Roberto on the back and hugging him. Once they began to calm down and take their showers, Roberto sitting silently in front of his locker, was told by the team clubhouse attendant, someone wanted to see him in the hallway. Roberto got up slowly and prepared to find out what Juan and his underworld friends would do to him now, since he did not throw the game, as agreed. He walked out into the hallway, preparing to be shot on sight, but to his surprise, it was Mary standing with a short, muscular looking man in his late thirties or early forties. They smiled at Roberto, as Mary hugged him. Suddenly, Coach Perez emerged from the locker room and joined them.

"Roberto, this is my friend, *Señor Garcia*, my former teammate and the head of football at the *Universidad de Panama*." They shook hands formally. *Señor Garcia* said, "They will be talking about that shot for many years. Would you like to come to my school and shoot a few of those for me?"

Roberto smiled and answered, *"Si."*

After a few minutes of discussing Roberto's college future, they parted ways, with Roberto returning to his locker to ponder his future fate and why his soccer instincts had betrayed his rational mind at the last second. He didn't have to wait long, as the team attendant came once again to tell him someone was waiting to see him in the hallway.

Roberto rose up, and with a sigh, moved to the door. He was not surprised to see Juan standing there scowling at him. He moved quickly to where Roberto had stopped just outside the door. Looking around at the empty hallway, Juan suddenly grabbed Roberto by his collars and shoved him violently against the hard cinderblock wall. "We had an agreement," he whispered savagely. Roberto simply shrugged and smiled at him. "Sue me," he said. Juan released him and stepped back. "I'm gonna' do more than that, *pendejo*! I'm gonna' do more than that!" he said, with pure venom in his voice and stalked away.

Later that night, at dinner with his mom and dad, who had both come unexpectedly to his game, Roberto asked his dad if he could speak to him alone for a minute. Looking surprised, his mother, who had noted her son's seemingly sadness, even though he was the hero of the game and the toast of the city, looked quizzically at her husband, who shrugged and left the table with his son. They went out on the back porch, still hot and humid, in spite of the approaching evening, and sat down on a small stone bench facing the backyard jungle. Roberto, looking down at the ground, confessed everything to his father and how he was thinking about leaving Panama forever to save his life.

The elder *Señor Johannas Morales*, a man who possessed a great deal of wisdom, but had smothered it after the death of his young daughter many years before, sat back and said, "Ahhhh," as he wiped the evening sweat from his forehead. He thought about it for a few minutes, not saying anything. He had worked the Panama Canal for over twenty years and was not without his connections. He knew men who worked hard on the docks, but were always looking for extra money, and were not afraid of some blood and sweat-for a price, of course. *Johannas* looked at his son, who he loved dearly, realizing he could have been a better dad and should have been there a little more for him growing up, made a quick decision.

"Roberto, give me the details of these men who may pursue you and I will have it settled with them." Roberto looked up at his father, with hope in his eyes.

"Really *Papa*? How?"

"Do not worry, my son, it will be taken care of and then you can go to the University, get an education and play soccer for them. Maybe make the National or the Olympic Team! Who knows, eh?"

For the first time in weeks, Roberto had hope, blinking rapidly with happiness.

"Now go talk to your mother about school and your future education, so that she will not feel she has been left out. She loves and misses you. It is time we heal together as a family! Yes?"

"*¡Gracias papá!*"

"And no more gambling! Agreed?"

"*¡Sí papá! ¡Te amo, papá!*"

In Johannas Morales' mind, the matter was simple. He called up two of his friends-big, tough dock workers named Geovanny and Fritz, who he knew needed money. He explained the situation, but, prudently, didn't tell them everything. In fact, so as not to incriminate himself, he told each of them a slightly different story. He also told them to play this one close to the vest and to not ask too many questions. The money would be good and the situation safe-at least as safe as any situation could be that could accidentally wind up in death. He met them at the docks that very evening, told them the rest of the plan, and gave them each $500.00 U.S. dollars. The only instructions he gave them, were, "Don't kill him, but beat him within an inch of his life, and put the fear of God in him. I don't want my family bothered again!"

The men, grateful for the work and, because Johannas was considered an "important man," on the docks, were honored he had entrusted this task to them. They would not fail him. Together, they drove over to Juan's house. The men stayed in the car, while Johannas knocked at Juan's door. Juan came out, not knowing who this unexpected visitor was, who knocked at his door, despite the late hour. The sun had just set and there was still a small amount of evening light left.

"What is it you want?" asked Juan.

"I am Roberto's father and I wish to speak with you."

Juan, bigger, tougher and younger, smiled at this *stupido* stranger. "Your son cost me a lot of money today. I am going to kill his ass! What are you going to do about it?"

"I would like to make a payment to you, so that his life is not held in forfeit. He has a good future ahead of him and I don't want it spoiled by the likes of you and your ilk."

"Ha, ha! You will owe me $10,000 US dollars, then. And then I will come back for more later!"

Johannas nodded weakly. "The money is in the car. You can come and get it, as this place frightens me and I wish to be away from here quickly."

Juan smiled and followed him to the car. It was all too easy. The bet was only for $8,000, but he thought Roberto's dad was an easy mark. See how he walked back to his beat-up car with his head down! He thought, *"¡El es un perdedor al que derrotaré!"* (He is a loser that I will defeat!)

Just as they got to the car, both of the back doors flew open and the dock workers jumped out. One of them grabbed Juan and pinned him up to the car, while the other began to beat him without mercy. Then, Johannas, holding a small club, resembling a policeman's night stick, hit him on the outside of his left knee, causing Juan to scream in pain. He then punched him in his testicles with the club, producing more screams. Both of the dock workers were working faster now. They punched him in his face and his body over and over again. One of them would hold Juan against the car while the other beat him, and then they would change places, so he would present a better target and not collapse on the ground. They were big men and their punches carried the weight of professional boxers. Neighbors began to look out of the windows of their small houses in this rural neighborhood. No one ventured out, as they all knew their neighbor was a bad person, and there were often shady characters who came and went to his house late at night. Most thought he was finally getting his due for some illegal drug deal that went bad.

Juan begged for mercy as the men beat him to a pulp. Two other small, mousy looking men came running out of Juan's house to try and help him, but after seeing the three men beating up their friend, they stopped short and retreated to the porch, looking on with fear.

Finally, Johannas told them to stop. Juan fell into a heap on the ground and, between moaning and crying, held his hands up, as if for protection, although the beating had stopped.

Johannes pulled out a wad of bills. He held them up in the air and then threw them on the ground next to Juan's head which was now lying on the pavement. Blinking rapidly, he looked up at Johannas.

"Johannas said, "This should do nicely. There's a grand. That settles it between you and my son. He won't be bothered again, or the next time we have to come back, you will simply disappear, *comprende*? I know your family. Why does a nice boy from nice parents, come to an end like this? In any event, I hear they are taking volunteers for the Army. Perhaps you should go back inside and re-think your life. Otherwise, your mother and your father will soon weep over your grave and wonder where they went wrong." He hesitated and then said, "That would be sad for them."

With that, Geovanni and Fritz grabbed Juan's almost lifeless body and dragged him away from the car. They jumped into the back seat and roared off into the steamy night air.

CHAPTER TWO

THE JOURNEY TO PANAMA AND THE DARIÉN GAP

THAT NIGHT, JAZMINE PARIS TOLD HER parents she had been selected for the trip to Panama to teach English to the local children. She had produced papers for them to sign, which lay silently on the family table in their home. Jack Paris, her father, thought Panama was a long way from their home in Danville, California and maybe a little too dangerous.

They were all eating Mexican food, their favorite, purchased from a local *Cantina*, and was as close to perfect as food could be. Unfortunately, neither Jack, nor his wife Lisa could taste anything. Jazmine was bubbly as ever, especially as she sensed her parents' dread of letting her go into the jungles of Panama. Her younger brother dug into his food and seemed oblivious to all of the drama.

Finally, Jazmine said to her mom and dad, "So is this going to happen, or are you both going to tell me to pass on this opportunity?"

Jack and Lisa exchanged glances. Lisa spoke up first. "I hear there is a group going over to Florida to teach English to Cuban Nationals who have immigrated to the U.S. It's doing the same service, but on U.S. soil."

The comment hung in the air for a long time. Jazmine was not going to give up so easily. "Dad, you had adventures in Columbia and in the Caribbean. I want to see the world too!" she added emphatically.

Jack glanced over at Lisa, but did not raise his head from his food. He chose his words carefully. "Yes, Honey, I went to exotic places, but it was not a picnic. I had to do bad things to bad people, just to stay alive-memories that will haunt me for the rest of my life!"

Jazmine continued, "He guarantees we will be safe. He has brought down multiple students to the area, and always returned them safely over the years. I really don't think there is anything to worry about!"

Jack sighed. "Let me talk it over with mom tonight and we will discuss it tomorrow. Can you please ask *Señor Roberto* to call us tomorrow to talk about our concerns?"

Jazmine nodded her head emphatically. "OK dad! Thank you!" She excused herself and ran upstairs to text and the rest of her friends who would be going on the trip.

Jack and Lisa talked about it late into the night. There was only one conclusion: let her go ahead with the group to Panama. They had sent a text to Señor Roberto, who agreed to meet them at a local café in Danville, to discuss the trip and safety measures that would be in place.

They met with him the next day and instantly trusted him. He was a person who inspired faith. Roberto's demeanor was professional and he assured them that he had made several of these trips in the past, always without incident. He told them there was nothing to worry about and provided the phone number of his cousin who worked in the *Consulados de Panama*. He encouraged them to check this reference if they had any doubts about his sincerity or the student's safety. "The government of Panama is anxious to maintain good relations with the United States and these 'outreach programs' are essential to promoting excellence in education and cooperation between the two countries," he added.

After a second long night of discussion, made all the more palatable by the fact that her resume' would be enhanced by this voluntary trip to help the poor and impoverished of a transcontinental country, Jack and Lisa signed off on the papers. They wrote a check for $1,200.00 to cover her round-trip plane fare, room and board for the 10 days, and gave her another $500.00 for additional expenses, such as some little treasures she may want to bring back with her.

One week later, Jack and Lisa drove their daughter, Jazmine to San Francisco Airport for her trip to Panama. and the other families met them at the terminal with the rest of the students, where everyone spread out their luggage on the ground inside the waiting area, before they went through the TSA station. They wanted to have everything organized. There were four girls, all seniors at the high school. took charge and allowed all of the parents to say good-bye to their children. Before too long, it was time to go through Customs and everyone said good bye, blowing kisses, as they walked through the terminal to the check point. That's when Lisa Paris turned to Jack and began to sob uncontrollably into his arms. "She's not coming back Jack! She's not coming back! What are we going to do about it?" She pulled back and looked into his eyes, "Jack! Fuck, Jack! She's my baby girl! Do something!" Lisa's voice was rising.

"Shhh. Shhh," said Jack. He was looking around at the people passing by and felt about as ineffective as a toddler trying to defend a three-point shot against Steph Curry.

"The fucking plane hasn't left the ground yet. What do you want me to do?!" he whispered. "Do you want me to drag her out of Customs and bring her home to Mommy and Daddy? That would leave a permanent scar! Jesus, Lisa!" He had never seen her act like this before.

Lisa kept crying. She was at a loss and then suddenly transformed into a momma lioness, protecting her cub. "Please call Bill Treese. Call John Waales. Ask them to go there and look after her. They are working down there somewhere. They can make sure she is safe. John is her Godfather, after all. He won't mind!" Her eyes were desperate, as she looked pleadingly at her husband. Jack nodded. "OK, OK!" he said.

****

Jack Paris, a chiropractor, who, because of events that had happened in his past, mostly on the PT boat, had seen more death and destruction in the past several years in South America, and the truth be known, some of it at his own hands, was understandably less confident. The truth was, he feared for Jazmine's life. Following Lisa's meltdown at the airport, he contacted his best friend,

Professor John Waales, Professor of Archaeology at U.C. Berkeley. John was working in Jamaica, helping his friend catalogue many rare antiquities discovered the prior year. Jack told John about his and Lisa's misgivings about Jazmine teaching English in Panama. After a lengthy discussion, Jack asked, "So, John, are we just being paranoid parents or what? They just left a few hours ago, and their teacher seems to be above reproach. He has years of experience bringing other kids there without incident."

John Waales, standing in the middle of an Archaeology Library, just outside of Kingston, Jamaica, flanked by piles of dusty open ancient books, scratched his head. He was not sure what to say. Finally, he replied, "Jack, what is your gut feeling on this? If other students have gone before, returned safely and all of the other parameters are the same, what's your concern?"

"It's mostly Lisa. You know, Mamma Bear has her radar up and her antennae are going off overtime. She doesn't like it and I almost had to drag Jazmine off the plane before it even took off!"

"So, do you think taking the PT boat crew going over to Panama or Colombia might make a difference?"

Jack sighed, "I don't know John. I was, actually, well, we were hoping you guys might be in the vicinity, just in case we, uh, you know…" his voice trailed off.

John thought a minute, "Let me talk to Bill. We might have business in or near Colon, Panama after all, which would put us pretty close to where she is supposed to be teaching."

Jack closed his eyes, gratefully. "Thanks John. Let me know ASAP, please!"

"OK, buddy. Let us know when they land and what is happening. They're supposed to be there ten days, right?"

"Right. I'll call Bill and talk to him as well. Is he there with you?" asked Jack.

"No, he's on his boat, but tied up to the dock. We were planning on shoving off in a couple of weeks to search for a lost treasure ship not too far from Cartagena, as a matter of fact. So, we will be heading in that direction anyway, and leaving early shouldn't be a problem."

"Thanks John!" Suddenly Jack, overcome with emotion, broke the connection and called for Lisa to come into his study to discuss what was going on.

Jack and Lisa talked for over an hour. Jack wanted to fly down to Panama, but Lisa, again questioning her own judgement, shook her head and said they needed to wait and hope she would just come back safely. She was very happy that the crew of the PT boat was going to travel near where the girls were going to be, because that made her feel a little safer.

Jack made his next call to his friend Bill Treese, the captain of the PT 109, normally based out of the Amazon River. Now, however, he had been working between Jamaica and the Brazilian Coast for the past year, helping a friend start a new grammar school. Jack couldn't raise him by cell phone, so he went next door and used his neighbor's shortwave radio to contact Bill's boat.

Bill Treese was tied up to the dock at Kingstown Jamaica. He had been there a year, on and off, and then had come back because he, John, John's daughter, Kimmi, and Bill's two mates on board, Manolo and Miguel were supposed to ship out to search for a lost sunken treasure ship, near Cartagena. He had been making preparations for them to leave in 10-14 days, depending on the weather. A storm was coming in over Central America, which would be windy and wet, but not of hurricane force – at least that was what the reports said.

Suddenly, Bill's radio cracked to life. "PT 109, this is Jack Paris. Please come in, over." The message was repeated, until Bill grabbed the microphone.

"Jack, Jack, good to hear from you! What's up? How can we assist, over?"

"Bill, good to talk to you! I'm on a friend's short-wave radio, here in California. John says you're still in Jamaica. Is that right, over?"

"*Ya, mon,*" Bill teased in a Jamaican accent. "What's up Jack, over?"

"Bill, has John talked with you yet, about my situation up here, over?"

"Yes Jack. John already called me. I've already spoken to my crew, Kimmi, Miguel and Manolo, the whole lot of us. We're ready to help out any way we can, over?"

"Bill," Jack's voice trailed off and he didn't think that he could continue.

"Jack, speak up! What's wrong with ye. It doesn't sound like there is anything to worry about, at least for now, over?"

"Bill, John probably told you my daughter, Jazmine, his Goddaughter, who was going down to Panama to teach English at a private school for ten days. Is it possible you can rendezvous with her near Colon in ten days? Would that be OK, over?"

"Of course, Jack. Don't be stupid! Over." Bill smiled, knowing Jack's reaction might make him angry, but this time, it surprised him.

In a timid voice, Jack said, "Thank you Bill, over."

Bill suddenly alarmed, said, "Hey buddy, I was just kidding! Are you seriously afraid for your little girl? It sounds like she will be OK, but if not, I will personally deal a blow to anyone who messes with my family. And you are now my family, after all we've been through! Over."

Jack closed his eyes and smiled. "Thanks Bill. I knew I could count on you. I'll send you the coordinates and tell her and her friends to meet the boat in ten days! I'm out."

Bill set the microphone down and, sitting in the charthouse, the communication center of the PT boat, thought for a long time. He knew they trafficked girls down here, but was Jack's daughter next? Why the sudden concern, when the school authorities were probably on this? Why would the people who commit these crimes, ever risk taking a bunch of high school girls, especially American high school girls on a teaching mission, when runaways were much easier pickings? Especially from California, one of the most populated states in the Union? Crazy! Too much risk for a few more stolen girls. If it was true and it happened, there would be hell to pay.

He knew hostages were moved through the Darién Gap, between Panama and Colombia, believed to be the most dangerous jungle in the world. There was a river that was accessible from the Caribbean side, known as the Atrato River. It was a shallow, brown waterway, meaning there were no deep channels, that would allow deep draft ships to pass. Smugglers were known to kidnap women and children, take them through the jungle, sometimes along or across the river, and then into Colombia. From there they were dispersed throughout South American and often throughout the world.

Bill hoped and prayed they were 100% wrong about this trip and Jack's daughter. Because, if something did happen, he had no idea where to start looking for missing girls from California. Another cluster, sent his way that he might have to deal with. He checked the charts and the weather and made preparations to leave sooner than he had planned. He made a call back to his friend Professor John Waales to discuss their impending mission.

****

The Atrado River starts in the Western Andres Mountain Range at almost 13,000 feet. It moves through the Chocó's jungle to the Caribbean Sea, near Panama. There are numerous tributaries feeding its muddy waters - over 15 other rivers and hundreds of streams. However, in spite of its pristine origin, it is one of the most contaminated rivers in the country, from people, gold mining and deforestation. Illegal gold mining excavations produce polluting sediment and erosion. However, it is one of the most important rivers to the Chocó people, who depend on its waters for their very survival. The Columbian Constitutional Court decreed that the Atrato River required better care and won widespread support for its protection and conservation. It is hoped this will lead to better management and eventually full restoration. In essence, the government wants the Atrato River to be cleaned up and seeks to build a new economy around it.

While the people who live on the river are in favor of this, there are other people in conflict with the decree.

The river itself, spans over 400 miles and passes through many dangerous, although beautiful biodiverse regions. There are constant illegal activities on this river from mining, logging, smuggling and deforestation activities. Caught in the middle are many inhabitants whose only intent is to survive and raise their families. They must be wary of these smugglers, but also be afraid of the internal strife due to the over fifty years of internal conflict between the local guerrilla forces and the Columbia's paramilitary groups, who use the Atrato River as their passageway and also to terrorize the peaceful people of the river. The guerrillas use the river to move their troops into position to attack and repel their enemies.

Adding to the river's notorious reputation, the military has also taken bribes from covert groups to help them move their human cargo, drugs and illegal contraband down river from its source to the Caribbean. Illegally mined gold is especially coveted, since the world gold prices rose significantly in the 2000's. When extreme mining is conducted with little oversight, profits are to be made by everyone, at least in the short term, until the ore mines play out. Sadly, because of this, the water and the surrounding vegetation suffers.

Poisonous mercury, used as an extraction method for gold, has caused many environmental and health problems, further contaminating the Atrato River. Solid waste present in the form of metals left behind as residue contaminates that affect the minor's health, as the mercury may enter their bodies through the fish they eat and also by direct skin contact while mining in the river.

More challenges exist, as the Chocó Rainforest spans from the northwest coast of the Andes mountains from southern Panama, through Columbia and into Equador. The rainforest is constantly under attack from people who want to clear cut the trees by illegal logging. This is a threat to the hundreds of species of birds, reptiles and other mammals who are native to the area and are not found anywhere else. Many organizations have been set up to preserve the rainforest, even in spite of the odds of success and also facing the danger of the constant warfare between the various factions fighting to control the area. The drug cartels and the government are fighting, with the local, poverty inflicted villages caught in between. Those that are native to the area know that this rainforest and its survival are paramount to the survival of the entire region.

****

General De Luna took his boatload of women to the Isthmus of the Darién River. There, they were promised they would be transported to Cartagena, where they could supposedly call their relatives and arrange for a fair ransom demand and passage back to their homes. In reality, none of this happened. Instead, they were grabbed by several soldiers and taken by force to a makeshift medical clinic.

Once inside, they were forced to strip and submitted to humiliating medical exams, testing them for venereal disease, autoimmune diseases, and anything else that would bring less than top dollar from the clients of General De Luna's bosses. The Cartel was mostly made up of Communists, but also had a hold in the governments of Colombia, Panama and Brazil. The Government bribed bureaucrats had a hand in producing certain documents which needed to be signed in order to make the transactions to appear legal, and then passed them on to the next level.

After their exams, the women, still naked, were led to a group shower, where they were ogled by the grinning soldiers. The soldiers had strict orders, on pain of death, not to molest the women. They were too valuable to be used for mere soldier's pleasure. The women were then taken to individual cells, where prisoner uniforms were handed to them. A woman soldier accompanied General De Luna into the cells. They discussed among themselves, the exam findings, as well as the overall attractiveness and "spirit" of each of them. The more attractive, the higher the price. The more belligerent, and spirited, then possibly the higher the price, as some customers liked to "break in" their women. Some of the girls, who were not particularly pretty or talented, would be sold off as servants. No one in this group would make them rich. They were mostly average, but would fetch a profit, which would please his bosses.

This world, thought General De Luna, is *an ugly place.*

He left the cells and was summoned by one of his guards. "What is it "Effy?" he asked.

"Communications from Panama, sir. They will be collecting four eighteen-year-olds from California," he paused, "All pretty, especially one who is a natural blond!" The right girl could sell for as much as one million U.S. dollars to a rich Sheikh or multimillionaire playboy in South America.

General De Luna smiled and looked out over the darkened city. *¡Mucho dinero!* he thought.

CHAPTER THREE

KIDNAPPED

JAZMINE PARIS HAD A FANTASTIC TIME teaching the Panamanian children English. She and her three friends had over one hundred students from five to thirteen years-old. They had held their classes both indoors and outside in the jungle clearings. The girls had all stressed the importance of making the classes fun and related to what was going on in the world now, rather than it be a boring history lesson. The result was lively classes full of fun and encouragement where the children were free to ask questions and speak their minds. As the week progressed, the students became bolder in their queries about life in the United States. They were fascinated about Americans and what their culture was all about. Food, clothing, dating, school-nothing was off limits. The girls were eager teachers, as they were truly excited about their own culture and were happy to share with their enthusiastic audience.

One girl named Claudia Archuletta, asked Jazmine what

it was like to be in the United States and be able to go to stores to buy designer jeans, make-up and Lululemon tops whenever she wanted. Jazmine replied that it was nice, but designer goods were so expensive, and that she could never buy everything she wanted. Claudia was thirteen, and almost the same size as Jazmine. So later that evening, Jazmine took a pair of her Gucci skinny jeans to Claudia's house on the edge of the rain forest. She knocked at the door and Claudia answered, surprised to see Jazmine. When Jazmine handed her the jeans, she protested loudly, but Jazmine, who had anticipated this, simply hugged her and asked her to please remember her and to do something nice for someone else down the road. Claudia nodded her head and, clutching the jeans close to her, ran back into her house as she began to cry. Jazmine didn't know that Claudia's father, Major Nando Archuletta, was actually a high commander in the Panamanian Army, with the means to buy his daughter such clothes, but refused to engage with the Black Market low-lives who sold them. So, when she came into the house looking so pleased, he was very happy for her and asked who the nice American girl was.

This small encounter, set up a plan in Jazmine's mind. She vowed someday to bring designer clothes to the girls and boys in this region, so that they could enjoy some of the finer things in life. She knew that on the surface, designer jeans were of little consequence compared to having enough food and protection from the bandits in the area. But what was the harm in a few poor girls and boys, getting some clothes they had only seen in magazines or on the internet? Anyway, she thought it would be a worthy effort and planned to pursue this dream someday.

The ten days flew by and before they knew it, it was time

to head back to the United States. They had been in contact with their parents and everyone was excited to return home and to tell their stories to their family and friends. Their last evening was going to be dinner at a local cantina. *Señor Roberto* had contacted the owner and had asked him to make sure they were going to have a fantastic celebration on their last night.

Gathered around the cantina's indoor picnic tables, Jazmine sat next to Jackie, a girl whose parents were from Puerto Rico. She was dark and exotic looking, the polar opposite of blonde and blue-eyed Jazmine. Next to them was Gwendolyn, who was half black and half white. She had green eyes, and was very pretty, sweet and demure. Last was Cazzy. She was a full bodied, brash brunette and very forceful. One might say her features were extremely cute, as opposed to beautiful. She owned the conversation at the table and spoke Spanish almost as well as Jazmine.

Because they were all 18 years old, the local drinking age, allowed them to have a couple of drinks each, but no more than that. As *Señor Roberto* explained to them, "I am responsible to your parents for your safety. You may have a little to drink, but you cannot have any more than that, or I will be in trouble!"

The girls all giggled and they all got up to hug him good naturedly. *Señor Roberto,* for his part, noted that everyone was having fun, but knew it was getting late and they needed to get back to their hotel soon. They were supposed to see Jazmine's godfather the next morning and get a ride on the World War II PT boat he was working on. They were going to cruise for a few hours, then they would head to the airport for an evening return flight to the

United States. Quietly, and between rounds, the bartender slipped the girls and *Señor Roberto,* a Mickey Finn into their cocktails, which would make them drift off into unconsciousness. *Señor Roberto's* was much stronger, as they needed for him to be out of the way first and in a deep coma-like sleep.

After an hour, the last of the girls fell asleep, with their heads on the table. The bartender got up and took each one's pulse. They were all steady and in perfect rhythm. He signaled to the other men in the bar. A truck was brought up to the back and the girls were carried outside and loaded into it. The steel door at the back of the truck was lowered and they drove off into the dark jungle night. Next, they brought out Señor Roberto and laid him down in a second truck. A man in uniform came out of the shadows. He walked up and looked down at *Roberto.*

Two military men approached him and saluted, "General Velasco, sir! We are ready to transport this man into the jungle to do what you wish."

The General, Juan Velasco, stood looking at their unconscious prisoner. He leaned down and whispered into *Señor Roberto's* ear, "I've waited 17 years for this moment, *Roberto.* Welcome home, *Putah!*"

****

To the parents, at first, everything was good. The students and had landed and were transported to the town where they were to teach the children English. They had all been in contact with their parents and everyone was happy, even Lisa Paris, who began to regret her outburst at the airport. But suddenly, after 10 days, communication went dead. Repeated calls to the girls went unanswered. The other parents checked with one another and confirmed not one of the girls was responding. Jack and Lisa had tried to call Jazmine over a dozen times, but she was not answering. Because there was a storm in the area, Jack was unable to contact either Bill Treese or John Waales, either by phone or radio. He suspected they were near either Colon or Cartagena, but he didn't really know.

It was now apparent that something was seriously wrong. The parents began to call the school administrators, demanding answers. The principal arranged a meeting at the high school for early the next morning.

In the auditorium, were eight worried parents, including Jack and Lisa Paris. The Principal, John Sugarman, Vice Principal, Harry Jones, Dean of Women, Melissa Gilbert, school nurse, Gretta Johnson and District Superintendent James Truedale, were in attendance.

Mr. Sugarman, spoke first, "We know you are all concerned about your children, and so are we. We have been in contact with the U.S. Embassy in Panama and they are investigating. They have requested the cooperation of the National Government and the local police force. They have also contacted the Colombian Government, just to cover their bases."

Lisa Paris, no shrinking violet, said, "Has anyone of you tried to contact *Señor Roberto?* He was the one who guaranteed their safety! Were the hell is he now?"

The principal said, "We have been trying to contact him. We are all concerned. The atmospherics have been challenging because of the many storms in the area, but we are still trying constantly." He continued, "Other than that, we are helpless to do anything more." He shrugged as though the situation was hopeless.

One of the other parents spoke up bluntly, "Nobody gives a flying shit about your "atmospherics!" Make a fucking phone call, for Christ sakes! Call the Embassy! Call the government! Call their fucking Marines! Get our children the hell out of there!" He fell back into the arms of his wife and they both began to sob.

The room was uncomfortably silent. Suddenly Jack Paris stood up. Lisa Paris grabbed his arm, but he shrugged it off angrily. He burned with a deep-seated anger at himself, not his wife, who wanted him to keep Jazmine from boarding the plane in the first place. *His wife was right-as always,* he thought, ruefully.

"My name is Doctor Jack Paris," he began. Since there have been no reported hurricanes, flood or fires, it's likely, that our daughters have been kidnapped, or 'Taken' as alluded to in a recent popular movie. If that is true, they will be sold into slavery, and it is likely your teacher is to blame, or at least may have had some part in this."

Jack looked directly at the five administrative officials of the school. "It's obvious that you idiots have been too wrapped up in your academic world to understand the ways of the REAL WORLD! You have no idea, what it's like to be down in South America, fighting for the safety of our families!" He paused, "But I do. Criminals down there are ruthless and stop at nothing. You can never be sure if the military and the politicians are trustworthy. This requires COVERT action. Action that I am no stranger to. I am going down there and I intend to bring back our children with the help of some close friends. I don't need your help. I don't want your cooperation. I do want to make it PERFECTLY clear that NONE OF YOU attempt to interfere with me. If you call the government, the State Department, the FBI, the A.T.F., or anyone else, and they interfere with me and my mission," he paused for almost 30 seconds, while everyone in the room shifted uncomfortably and held their breath, "Then our daughters will likely be lost forever and I will hunt you down and ruin your lives." He paused again and looked each one in the eye, "Every one of you." He rose and placed his hand out to Lisa. He turned to the other parents, "Trust me. I'll bring our babies back home." He and Lisa walked out into the cold, overcast morning and began to make their phone calls.

****

That night, after making what seemed like a hundred phone calls, Jack Paris sat down in the chair in his library, hoping to doze off for a couple of hours before he once again tried to book a plane flight to Panama. Suddenly, his phone rang. He could see by the dim light of his phone that it was Bill Treese. It was 10:15 P.M.

He hit the accept button and, closing his eyes at what he expected the answer to be, said, "Hi Bill. Any word?"

"Jack! We waited at the rendezvous point, but the girls never showed up! What do you want us to do? We can wait here or go look for them?

"Where are you, Bill?" asked Jack.

"We're in Colon, Panama. They never showed up." Bill's voice was rising. Everyone's nightmare was beginning to unfold.

Jack sat back in his office chair. He closed his eyes and leaned backwards. He heard Lisa enter the room. He knew what he had to say.

"Bill, we're pretty sure she's been taken by someone down there, maybe slave traders, along with the other three girls that she came down with. They had a chaperone, a *Señor Roberto*, who is also missing. We don't know, but he may have betrayed them. No one is answering their phones. We called his cousin who works in the *Consulates of Panama* down there and he hasn't heard anything either. He vehemently denied his cousin could be a part of this, but we're not so sure. We think their government is trying to keep this quiet, because they don't want any bad publicity with the U.S. I can't get a flight down there until next week due to the storms and the unstable air. Everything is grounded. I don't know what to do." Jack Paris put his head into his hands as his wife, Lisa put her arms around him.

"Jack," said Bill, "Why don't you call Charlie? She is a pilot and may be willing to help."

Jack shot up with a rush of adrenaline. "Great idea! Thanks Bill. I'll call you! Wait, what's her phone number?"

"Hell," said Bill, "I don't know, but she lives near you. Take a drive to that community she lives in and ask around! I'll be in touch," and with that, Bill hung up.

CHAPTER FOUR

CHARLIE AND ZENADIA

JACK DIDN'T KNOW CHARLIE'S PHONE number, but he knew she lived in the exclusive Blackhawk community in Danville, California. He decided to just drive the few miles to her neighborhood. Charlie had been part of Bill and Jack's previous adventure, looking for the Lost El Dorado. She was a retired Air Force pilot and Viet Nam Vet, who had worked with Bill Treese during the war. She was still typed in jets and owned one she kept at Buchannan Field in Concord, California. Jack had flown with her once before.

Jack ran back into the bedroom to change clothes. He turned to Lisa, "I need to go to Blackhawk and see Charlie right now." Lisa nodded, and he ran downstairs, out the back door and into the garage.

Jack jumped into his red 1976 Porsche Targa, and roared off into the night.

In less than 15 minutes, he was pulling up to the West

Gate at Blackhawk. He had to wait a few minutes while two cars ahead of him, seemed to be taking their time getting in through the controlled gate. Finally, the cars moved, and Jack was facing the gate guard who looked none too friendly, maybe because of the lateness of the hour or the fact that Jack was in a sports car, and looked out of place in the Visitor's Lane.

The man at the gate, was named Victor and he was Swiss-American. Blond haired and blue-eyed, he was a clandestine, strong-arm soldier, and was aware of every movement here in Blackhawk. Strangely enough, he had been an Israeli soldier but was now fighting for an army bitterly opposed to Israel and their current policies. He was here on assignment, to track certain high-level executives in this East Bay City. At the top of his list was Charlie, who was worth close to one billion dollars. Also, he had been informed three weeks ago about the impending kidnapping of the girls in Panama. His superiors were customers of Jazmine's captors and potential buyers of the girls. His briefings instructed him to be wary of anyone who showed up looking for Charlie, especially if they looked out of place.

Jack's Porsche was flashy. It had a Whale's Tail, soft top, and huge tires. Jack had the top down, open to the night.

"Can I help you sir?" asked Victor professionally.

Jack Paris held out his business card and handed it to the guard. "My name is Dr. Jack Paris. I would like to see Charlie. I don't have an appointment."

Victor took Jack's card and scrutinized it. "Charlie?" he asked.

Jack panicked. He did not know Charlie's last name.

"Uh, uh," he stammered.

"Shit, I don't know! Should I call someone?" he asked. "She has a daughter named Zenadia. I know that!"

Victor smiled. He knew exactly who Jack was asking for, but he didn't want to give anything away. He was actually on a mission. This was an important part of his quest, and he had finally gotten a piece of the puzzle.

"Wait a moment sir. I will try to assist you!"

Victor pulled up the Blackhawk list of residents on his computer and rang Charlie's home phone.

Jones answered on the first ring. "Yes. This is Jones. May I help you?"

"This is Victor at the gate."

"Yes sir."

There is a gentleman in a Porsche named Dr. Jack Paris and he seems most anxious to see Ms. Charlie. Shall I send him up or call the police to have him removed, sir?"

"Wait a moment, please," he said curtly. After two minutes, Jones came back to the phone. "Ms. Charlie would like to see Dr. Jack Paris immediately. Please let him proceed, and please give him the directions to the estate."

"Yes sir."

"Thank you."

Victor gave Jack the address and told him to proceed to Charlie's house. As Jack drove away, Victor watched him and made a call on his cell phone.

Jack drove at the speed limit, which was slow, because he knew this was a gated and strictly controlled community. The last thing he wanted was a speeding ticket on his way to see Charlie. He and Lisa had looked at a property here early in his career and, while they found the community beautiful, with two excellent golf courses, Jack was already a golf member at the Olympic Club in San Francisco, and it just didn't make financial sense.

He arrived at a fairly nondescript house, considering the area, with an ornate entryway, which led up to several steps to the front door. He rang the doorbell. Almost immediately, the door was opened by a small mousy looking man. He bowed slightly as he made his introductions, "Hello sir, I am Jones. At your service sir."

Suddenly, Charlies' voice came booming out of the back, from another room.

"Is that Jack Paris? Where have you been the past year? You decide to call on me at 10:30 at night? What the hell, Jack?"

Jack looked down and smiled slightly. "Hi Charlie. Do I get to see you, or are you going to be like the Great OZ and talk to me from behind the green curtain?"

Suddenly Charlie appeared in front of Jack. She was tall, visibly strong, and looked like she was forty, in spite of being in her early 60's. Bare-footed, she had on a pair of light blue designer jeans and a tight-fitting black turtle neck top. She wore a heavy gold necklace which circled her neck, and very large diamond earrings hanging almost to her shoulders. She and Jack had gotten to know each other briefly last year.

"Nice to see you again Jack, it's been a while. Come up to the living room. There seems to be something amiss here. How can I help you untwist this situation you find yourself in, whatever it is?"

As they ascended the stairs into the ornate living room, flanked by the rich wall tapestries, marble floors, granite walls, and Persian rugs, Jack suddenly knew what it meant to live in the lap of luxury.

Charlie gestured for Jack to sit on a beautifully ornate couch, which faced a large window. They heard a small noise and both turned to see a young native girl approach them. She stopped in front of Jack and smiled at him.

"You remember my daughter Zenadia?" asked Charlie. "She is here to help us if needed."

Jack smiled at Zenadia, "Hi," he said with some reserve. The last time he had been with her was on a beach in Colombia, but they did not speak. Zenadia was dressed somewhat more demurely than he remembered. She was about 5 feet tall, with long, black hair, which cascaded wildly down her back almost to her buttocks. She had on a wrap-around skirt and a loose-fitting top, which was cut low in the front.

"So why are you here so late and how can we help you, Jack?" asked Charlie.

Jack looked down and did not answer at once. He began to silently cry, his tears falling to the living room floor.

Zenadia, alarmed, sat down next to Jack and embraced him, hugging him preciously, as though it was life or death.

Charlie, feeling somewhat left out, placed a hand on Jack's shoulder, even as Zenadia continued to hug him. "Jack, what's happening?" she asked, obviously concerned with Jack's sudden change in demeanor.

Starting slowly, Jack began to confess. "My baby. My daughter Jazmine is missing. We think she has been kidnapped and we know," he hesitated, "we think she will be sold into slavery. She went down to Panama on a mission to teach English to the locals, but now all communication with the group of girls she is with has stopped. Not a word from any of them, including their chaperone, who is a native of Panama."

Charlie took a deep breath. "Jack, that is an amazing story and one I am trying to process. Obviously, the academic people who run these charters should be aware of what is going on, but, really, how do you know all of this? Is the Panamanian government involved? Was it a private sojourn down there without official oversight? How long have they been missing? What is being done by the locals? Hell, they can't just disappear into thin air. Is it possible everyone is just panicking over nothing? I'm sorry, but I have to ask."

Jack nodded. "All reasonable questions. All understandable reasons to wait until we know something for sure. But, if they have been taken, you probably know as much as anyone, that we have a window of 24-48 hours to find them, or they will likely be lost forever." He looked up at Charlie, who was a veteran of both the Air Force and the C.I.A., "If anyone knows how this shit works it's you!"

Charlie nodded.

Jack continued, "I just need someone who can take me down to either Colon, Panama or Cartagena, not sure which yet, until I hear from Bill Treese."

"Bill Treese?" asked Charlie. "How is he involved?" Jack noted the gleam in her eye. Forty years ago, Bill and Charlie were shipmates and lovers. They had been estranged due to events beyond their control for many years.

"Bill, John and the rest of the crew of PT 109 were in Jamaica, because we met some people there last year and he helped them out. I contacted him and he said they were actually getting ready to go and explore a sunken wreck off Cartagena, which is not terribly far from where the girls were teaching classes in Panama. He was going to Colon to meet up with my daughter and the girls before they flew home. But of course, they didn't show up and there is no trace of them. We have a few hours to locate them, or they will likely be gone forever. I am hoping you'll fly me down there and drop me off, because I can't get a commercial flight out due to the inclement weather. That can be the end of your involvement. I don't want to put you," he hesitated because Zenadia still clung tightly to him, which, strangely, warmed Jack's heart, as he knew what she had been like before, "or your daughter, Zenadia, in harm's way."

Charlie shook her head, "Jack Paris……. Jack, Jack, Jack! What happened to us a couple of years ago has changed my life," she hesitated and looked at Zenadia, "our lives, in ways you cannot imagine."

She looked down at Zenadia, who looked back up at her, smiled and nodded.

Charlie continued, "Sounds like you need a couple of really tough bitches to go down there and help you deal with a bunch of assholes!"

Jack raised a hand and started to protest, but Charlie cut him off, "No, no. I have saved Bill's ass plenty of times in country, and you can remind him of that fact when we get down there and get aboard his boat!"

Jack smiled. "I am sorry to bring this affair to you, but if you can help us, so much the better."

Charlie responded, by telling Jack go home to pack and

then meet them back at her house in two hours.

She and Zenadia would be ready.

In two hours, Jack was back at the estate. He had brought his telescoping metal nunchakus, metal stars for throwing, darts which would penetrate skin, and a short sword for fighting. He also had his Smith and Wesson AR-15, which could still be set for full auto if needed, strictly against California law, but he kept it hidden at all times.

Jack appeared at Charlie's doorstep with his military backpack ready to go. He was dressed in military, jungle fatigues, with heavy combat boots. Jones appeared and told Jack to please wait in the living room, as Charlie and Zenadia would be along shortly.

Jack sat on the same couch he had occupied earlier. He thought about the tearful goodbye he and his wife Lisa shared an hour earlier. Jack had gone home and told Lisa everything they planned to do. Naturally she wanted to go with him, but he convinced her to stay and keep their son company, who had just learned what was going on. He was terrified for his sister and knew their dad was going down to try to bring her home. Lisa made Jack promise to keep her informed of what was going on as much as he could. At last, just before he left, she hugged him, and they both cried.

"You better come back, Jack Paris, and bring our daughter home!" she said.

Jack nodded, "I will. I promise." He then slung his oversized back pack over his shoulder, picked up his heavy grip, and went down to the garage to return to Charlie's house.

Jack sensed, rather than heard Zenadia come into the

living room. She smiled at Jack. She was dressed the same as earlier, as though she was just going down to the grocery store or out shopping for clothes in a local mall.

"Where is your suitcase?" Jack asked.

"Jones already packed it in the car. My mom will be here in a minute."

There was an awkward silence for a few minutes. Finally, Jack asked, "How have you been, Zenadia? Are you OK now?"

Zenadia smiled again, "Of course."

"Zenadia, I'm not sure where to begin. I know we had a, uh, situation back in the El Dorado, but now I realize, uh, I really need your help."

Zenadia laughed, "Don't worry about it, Jack! I've already figured it out!"

After a pause, Zenadia asked him, "Do you think I am still a witch?" Startled at the directness of her question, he flinched and looked away from her for a second. He acted innocent and shrugged his shoulders. Zenadia smiled and said, "I'm no longer a bad girl, but I still have some of my powers from the old days. I'm not a witch, but maybe something that rhymes with it? HAHA! Pretty sure Mom and I can help you out."

"I can guarantee that, Jack!" They turned to see Charlie emerge in full battle fatigues. She was tall and strong; she inspired confidence, and Jack immediately felt better, happy with his decision to engage the two women.

Jack smiled, "I'm just glad we are on the same team this time!"

They went down to the garage where Jones took Jack's gear and placed it in the back of Charlie's 1937 Rolls Royce Phantom

III. They all climbed in and Jones drove out onto the dark streets of Blackhawk, California. It was after midnight. Once they were on the freeway to Concord's Buchanan Field Airport, Jack looked at the cars heading either to or from work, wishing he was simply going in to the office to adjust his patients, rather than flying to South America, once again, likely to do battle – but now the stakes couldn't be higher, as his daughter's life was in the balance.

Charlie interrupted his thoughts. She closed off the window between Jones in the front seat and the three of them in the back.

"Once we get to the plane, Jack, go ahead and go to the back. Strap in and try to get some sleep. We'll arrive late morning or early afternoon, depending on the winds aloft. Did you let Bill Treese know to meet us there?"

Jack nodded, already feeling tired, but too worried about Jazmine to be able to sleep.

"Then we will land and rendezvous with him and the boat. We'll find out what he knows and, if necessary, check in with the local authorities. I've already made some phone calls…." Her voice trailed off.

"Who did you call?" asked Jack.

Charlie smiled, "Don't worry about it."

Jack nodded and stared out at the thin traffic, as Jones whisked them to the airport.

****

Once the Rolls Royce drove out of the West entrance of Black Hawk, Victor, the guard at the gate, made a second call. Within a minute, a nondescript, black, newer model Chevrolet pulled up at the gate. An almost identical looking blonde haired, blue-eyed guard, dressed in exactly the same uniform as Victor, stepped out and entered the guard shack. Victor got in the back of the sedan. There was a change of clothes for him, plus a Sig Saur 9mm pistol and an AK-47 fully automatic machine gun.

There were two men in the front seat. Not a word was spoken as Victor changed into his battle fatigues, and then slipped into a pressurized flight suit. They drove to an abandoned airstrip in Concord, near the old Naval Weapons Station. As they pulled up one of the men in the front seat said, in a harsh Russian accent, "Do not fail us Victor!"

"да," (yes), he said without emotion, but staring straight ahead into the dark night, contemplating his mission. He was fluent in several languages.

They let him out and the sedan drove off quickly without lights.

Three more men stood in front of a retired, but refurbished Soviet jet from the Korean War. The Mikoyan-Gurevich MiG-15, was just over 33 feet in length and armed with 2x23 mm Nudelman-Rikhter NR-23 autocannons and 1x37 mm Nudelman N-37 autocannon. It originally had a maximum speed of 669 mph, but with newer technology modifications, including swept wings, it could achieve speeds close to Mach 1, and was highly maneuverable. Victor, nodded silently to the men, but said nothing. They did not acknowledge him in any way as he climbed into the cockpit, and made preparations to take off. He was monitoring local aviation traffic, planning to wait until Charlie's plane had taken off from Buchannan Fields, a few miles away.

The abandoned airstrip had not been used in years, and

from the air you could see a giant **X** covering it, warning pilots not to try to land on it due to its dangerous condition. Even now, Victor knew the black-top was rough with many broken chunks, which could cause a plane to veer off on its ground roll and crash prior to lift off. Victor knew his ground crew had been working to repair as much as they could, but he had to make a skilled roll out in spite of the condition of the runway.

He didn't have to wait long for Charlie, as he heard the chatter on the airway call out her plane's numbers as she took off. He waited 5 minutes and, firing up his jet engines, rolled out and took off into the night, trying to be as quiet as his jet would allow.

****

A few minutes earlier, at Buchanan Field Airport, Charlie's Rolls Royce pulled up to the East Ramp. Her Cessna Citation X was waiting. It normally had a top speed of Mach .935, but had been modified to go over Mach 1, which was the speed of sound. It also had a few other intriguing modifications.

Charlie, Zenadia and Jack walked over to the plane. Charlie's assistant, Akers, a tall, dark German gentleman, stood at the stairs leading up to the plane. He nodded politely, but said nothing. Zenadia took Jack by the hand and led him up the stairs and into the plane.

Once they were alone, Charlie turned to Akers. "Did you make the modifications I asked for?" Akers had been with Charlie for many years and was from West Germany, where he had studied advanced weaponry, under the auspices of the U.S. Government.

"Jawoll, mein Frau! Die waffen sind vorhanden, (The weapons

are in place).

"Danke, Akers!"

Akers smiled and nodded with a slight bow.

Charlie climbed up the stairs and settled into the cockpit. She began pressing buttons and turning dials. The engines fired up. She had owned this jet for many years and had made several modifications. It appeared to be a simple, fast civilian jet, but was fortified by machine guns and cannons, reflective of the jets she flew in the military. The guns were removed or added as needed, whether it was a journey to check on her real estate holdings or if she needed to fly a mission for the CIA, (who had kept her around for an occasional "project" that needed a delicate touch). Retirement and a clandestine, lucrative discharge from the Air Force had its advantages.

Charlie called Ground Control and asked for clearance to Runway 32 Right. She had filed a flight plan to Mexico City, but would modify it in the air. She didn't want anyone to know their real destination, at least for now.

She taxied out to the runup area for Runway 32 Right and made her preflight preparations.

"Tower, 787 Foxtrot Niner Niner, now in position for takeoff."

"Roger that," said the tower, "787 Foxtrot Niner Niner, you are cleared for takeoff."

"Rodger, tower." With that, Charlie pushed the throttle forward and the jet accelerated down the runway and lifted off into the early morning darkness.

Charlie and her crew, flew on a straight path toward

Colon, Panama. She expected to land early that afternoon. The flight was uneventful. Jack and Zenadia slept in the back of the plane in seats that folded down. Charlie was kept busy navigating, as she was entering the front of the storm that was enveloping Central America.

Victor was two hundred miles behind Charlie, but had her on his radar. He had to let her stay ahead of him. With intense determination, he followed Charlie into the storm, accepting that he was expendable, though his mission was not.

After five hours in the air, they passed the city of Reynosa, and moved toward the Gulf of Mexico. That was when Victor decided to attack.

Victor had tracked Charlie's jet at 27,000 feet, flying on an easterly heading, on Instrument Flying Rules, (IFR). He was 100 miles behind her, on the same heading. Believing he was evading her detection he wasn't worried about Charlie spotting him. He pulled up to 31,000 feet and moved ahead to only 25 miles above and behind Charlie.

Unbeknownst to Victor, Charlie had been tracking him for the past 500 miles. She was operating her stealth radar, and could see he was flying a MiG-15. *Slightly behind the times and place,* she thought. It had been tracking her for much too long to be a coincidence. Plus, coincidences were not part of her world or her C.I.A. training. When it came to combat, no one was better than Charlie – on land or in the air. She saw his sudden move to go to 4,000 feet above her, as he closed the gap between them. It was now or never.

Charlie pressed a button on her console which produced

a quiet *"Whoop, whoop, whoop,"* similar to battle stations on a navy vessel. Immediately Zenadia and Jack woke up and came up to the cockpit.

"What's happening?" asked Jack.

"We are going to be attacked in the next few seconds, by an ex-military plane, called a MiG-15. We are at Battle Stations. Zenadia, sit next to me. Jack, move back to the very rear of the plane. You'll see a seat there marked 'Hot seat'. Sit there, strap yourself in, and wait for me to tell you what to do. You will be safest there if we are shot at. Both of you put, on the parachutes and battle helmets stashed under the seats you were just in. Now move!"

Both Jack and Zenadia scrambled into position. In less than a minute, Zenadia returned and, sat in the Copilot's seat. She looked at her mother. "What do you want me to do?" she asked.

"Just stay with me and advise me. You still have your ability to see things and your instincts are intact. Whatever comes to your mind, if we are in for a dogfight, don't think about it. Just say or do immediately whatever you think of." She looked over at Zenadia, "Our lives might just depend on it!"

Zenadia nodded and began to focus her thoughts on the plane behind them. She went deep into her mind and brought the plane into view. Her thoughts swiftly came through the air, onto the MiG-15 and into the cockpit. She focused on the pilot. She gasped, "Oh my God!"

"What is it?" asked Charlie.

"It's that fucking guard from the guardhouse at Black Hawk! I told you every time I saw him, he was bad! He's trying to kill us!"

Just then, Victor dropped his left wing and moved in for the kill. His jet dropped, screaming through the sky! He tried to lock them up using his onboard radar, in its search and track mode. With a visual on Charlie's jet, he tried get her plane into his firing pattern.

Charlie yelled to Zenadia, "He is trying to lock us up and kill us. I can get us out of here, but can you do something that will distract him?"

Zenadia smiled. Although repentant from her Dark Side days, she still had many of her former powers.

Suddenly, diving out of the clouds, Victor opened up and fired on the Cessna, not expecting it to be anything else than a civilian transport vessel. As he was looking through the clouds, he began to see gigantic blue eyes staring at him, reflective of Zenadia, which blinded him momentarily. He put up his forearm over his eyes and tried to clear them. "Ah!" he said, as the pain burned into his eyes.

Charlie pressed the button on the console, and suddenly the Cessna went into "Combat Mode". She pulled back on the yoke and throttle, and the Cessna flew straight upward. Adding power, the plane was about to reach Mach 1, which would break the sound barrier. Unfortunately, neither Jack nor Zenedia were wearing pressurized flight suits, so Charlie couldn't risk it, as they could pass out if the pressure system in the jet failed.

Charlie dove her plane down, avoiding a machine gun volley from the MiG. She knew she couldn't simply evade Victor and had to counter attack. She brought her plane up and was able to get behind him. Opening her throttle, she chased him across the Gulf of Mexico, trying to lock him up on her radar fire control system. Using her fixed wing machine guns, she fired into his plane, but there was very little damage. They both scrambled to move into attack position.

Finally, Charlie, pulled back on her yoke, sent her Cessna straight up and then came screaming down, guns firing at the MiG-15. Victor, stunned and now mute, had no idea he was about to be shot out of the sky. Guns blazing, the Cessna found their mark as he tried to escape. But the MiG-15 was too slow. Bullets ripped part of the fuselage away and hit the engines. Smoke billowed from the crippled jet. Victor was going to bail out, but Zenadia appeared next to him, smiling and trying to comfort him. She touched his cheek and kissed him. He was enraptured by her beauty and her touch, never noticing he was about to hit the surface of the ocean, until it was too late. The plane exploded as it hit the water, sinking immediately below the surface and disappeared forever!

CHAPTER FIVE

ROGOMAN

BILL TREESE LOOKED AT THE CHARTS IN front of him. He was in a quandary. Tied up to the docks in Colon, Panama, the girls had not shown up as planned. He poured over maps of the city and the surrounding areas. This part of the country was not familiar to him. All he knew was that Jazmine and her friends were down here teaching, then they disappeared into the night, without a trace.

At that moment, John Waales came into the charthouse. "Hi Bill. Any luck?"

"Yeah, all bad. Did Jack tell you the name of the school where they were teaching English? I'd like to start there."

John pulled out an old notebook from his back pocket. While everyone else used their smart phones and electronic note pads, he still used paper and a pen to jot down his many notes and thoughts. He searched it eagerly, certain that Jack had told him.

"Yes! Bingo! Here it is. Queen of All Saints in Colon. It is a

Catholic charter school. They have many upper echelon children of the Panamanian elite, but then open their doors for many not so fortunate kids. They really try hard to bridge that gap and give everyone a chance to succeed in academic endeavors. Bringing our best students down to teach here is one of their top priorities. That really warms my heart as an academic!"

Bill looked at the map and punched it up on his computer, which had a satellite link up. He wrote the coordinates on a piece of paper.

"OK. Let's get the others together down in the galley and make our plans."

Bill and John descended the ladder in the small galley. John went into the forecastle to get his daughter Kimmi. She was sitting on her bunk talking to Manolo, one of Bill's mates. They had been a couple for over a year now. Bill hollered back into Miguel's stateroom, "Miguel, can you join us please?"

"Si, Capitain!"

Everyone gathered around the small table. Miguel, Kimmi and Manolo sat, while John and Bill stood. It was hot and humid. The storm was still raging outside, but the PT boat was tied up firmly to the dock. The guns were all lashed down, and the ordnance was locked away. Rubber bumpers protected the boat's hull from being pounded by the storm against the dock.

The PT boat was a fully-functioning, fully-restored WWII Pt boat. It was named PT 109, after John F. Kennedy's boat that was sunk in the Solomon Islands in June, 1943. JFK had survived and rescued most of his crew. Bill was Captain of a riverine boat in Viet Nam. He had rescued this PT boat, (which was a different number) off the scrap heap, purchased her and rebuilt her, after he was discharged from the Navy. He had sailed his boat down to the Amazon, and set up a business taking people out for trips up the Amazon River. He also transported legal cargo, but, despite many offers, declined to ever transport anything illegal. That's not how Bill was brought up. He was a big man, and very strong. He would never shy away from a fair fight, or a square deal. He never cheated anyone and was always a gentleman. His crew of Manolo and Miguel loved him, and he treated them more like his sons, rather than workers on his boat.

Bill addressed them all.

"We've been through a lot together situations on this boat over the past few years, but this may be our most challenging mission yet. Not only is our friend Jack's daughter missing, but she may have been taken by kidnappers who may sell her, as well as the other three girls she came down here with. I'm not sure how to handle this, but I think, together, we can come up with some ideas."

Kimmiko Waales spoke up. Jack was her Godfather, and he was also her dad, John's, best friend. "Is Uncle Jack flying down here?"

Bill nodded, "Yes with a couple of our old friends."

"Who?" Kimmi asked. Her dad smiled and looked away.

Bill also smiled. "Do you remember Charlie and Zenadia?"

Manolo, Miguel and Kimmi all turned around and looked at Bill at once. Manolo treas the first to speak, "That will be good for us! Those girls are really tough!"

"*Si,*" said Miguel, "I hear they are bad ass *Señoritas!*" They all laughed.

"We'll need all the help we can get," said Kimmi. "When

will they be here?"

"Later today," said Bill.

John asked, "So what do you want us to do in the meantime?"

"I would like for you, Kimmi and I to go to the school and speak to them about what they might know. It is such a bizarre situation. I hope they just sent them to a vacation island and that this is all just a silly mistake," said Bill.

Kimmi spoke up, "But you don't believe that, do you Uncle Bill?"

He smiled at his favorite "niece", the daughter of his closest friend. "No," he said simply.

"We'll leave Manolo and Miguel on the boat and we will go to the school to make some inquiries."

An hour later, Bill, John and Kimmiko were sitting in the headmaster's office, waiting for him to join them. They had been transported to the school by taxi, as the storm was beginning to ease up. Despite wearing Navy surplus foul weather gear, they were still pretty soaked. So, when they showed up at Queen of All Saints school, unannounced and asking to see the headmaster, there was some concern on the part of the secretaries. It was 10:00 A.M. and the children were in school. John introduced himself as a Professor of Archaeology from U.C. Berkeley, which helped, as there was always that mutual respect between academic institutions. John explained to the secretary that the girls who had come down from the United States were now missing and one of them was the daughter of a dear friend of theirs. The secretary was shocked and called for the headmaster to return from the class, where he was guest lecturing immediately. After a brief discussion over the intercom with the headmaster, she ushered them into what was probably his private office and asked them to please sit down on a large, brown leather sofa.

After about five minutes, the door opened and the three of them stood up. A smallish man with oversized black-framed glasses, dressed in black slacks, a white dress shirt, black tie, and a red sweater, came into the room. He extended his hand.

"I am *Señor Perez*. I am happy to meet you all. However, I am extremely concerned about what my secretary has told me about our guests from last week!" He gestured toward the couch they had been sitting on. "Please sit down and tell me what you know," he said with a strained look on his face.

They sat down on the sofa, and *Señor Perez* sat behind his desk in a large leather chair.

Bill, John and Kimmi looked at each other, not sure where to begin. Bill spoke up, "*Señor Perez*, we were going to ask you the same thing. Can you please tell us the last time you saw the girls and their chaperone, *Señor Roberto?*"

"Ah, yes," *Señor Perez* said. "They worked hard all week with our students. They were all kind, bubbly and so very sweet. Our students fell in love with them, as did we. They did an excellent job teaching English. We have people here who teach English, but the girls brought a sense of style and fun to our students. Plus, the feel of the United States and everything that comes with being an American." He smiled, "One girl in particular made a great impression on some of the girls here. She gave some of her American designer jeans to one of our students, who was very touched by her kindness. She vowed to come back and bring more nice clothes from the U.S., that we cannot buy here. Her name was Jazmine."

John spoke up immediately, "She's my Goddaughter and that sounds exactly like her!"

Señor Perez nodded respectfully.

Bill asked, "So what happened on their last day here?"

Señor Perez said, "They taught their final classes. Many of the students said goodbye and their chaperone, *Señor Roberto,* said he was going to take them out to eat to celebrate, before heading back to their hotel. Their plane was due to leave the next evening. I had no idea they never showed up. It is my fault for not following up with them." He looked down and shook his head.

"No," said Bill, "Not your fault. Do you know where they went to eat? That should be our next stop."

"No," said *Señor Perez,* " I have no idea. They could have gone anywhere."

John asked, "So the question is, did they made it to the hotel after their dinner? Or, if they went missing, was it on the way to the restaurant, or from it? Or maybe they were kidnapped in their sleep, or on the way to the airport?"

Señor Perez said, "I have no answers, because I have only just been made aware of this situation. But let me ask my secretary if she or anyone else knows where they might have gone to eat. That should be our first concern, to see if they showed up and, or if they left." He got up and left them in the room. Through the open office door, they could hear him talking in rapid Spanish to his secretary. She answered him and they spoke back and forth quickly. She pressed an intercom button and said something in Spanish to the person at the other end. After a minute, the person spoke back to the secretary.

John, Bill and Kimmi all could speak varying degrees of Spanish, but they had a hard time catching up to what was being said so rapidly. Finally, *Señor Perez* came back into the room and explained. "We contacted the main teacher, whose class spent the most time with the four girls. We did not tell her the reason, but simply asked if she or anyone in her class knew where they went to celebrate. The teacher said one girl, the one I told you about who liked Jazmine a lot and who, was given some of her clothes, said she knew and is on her way down here. She is a very bright girl and her father is an important Major in the Panamanian Army."

There was a timid knock on the door and *Señor Perez,* got up to answer it. As he opened the door, he said in Spanish, "please come in." A small, very pretty young girl, who was about 5 feet tall came into the room. She looked startled to see the two men and the young woman seated on the couch staring at her. Bill, John and Kimmi all stood up politely as she entered the room. She was immensely shy, but *Señor Perez,* spoke to her in Spanish for a few seconds and she relaxed a little.

Señor Perez made the introductions. *"Señor Bill, Señor John and Señorita Kimmiko,* may I present *Señorita Claudia Archuletta,* one of our brightest students and a friend to your Jazmine." They were about to shake her hand, but instead, Claudia did a little curtsey, as a formal greeting, which the three of them thought was very sweet and polite.

Señor Perez quickly filled Claudia in on why they were here. When he mentioned the girls were missing, her eyes flew open wide and her hand rose to her mouth, as if to stifle a scream. She started to cry, but *Señor Perez* said to her in Spanish that they needed to search for the girls and were in a huge hurry. She gathered herself up as best as she could. He asked her if she knew where they went to celebrate their last night and she nodded.

Señor Perez said in Spanish, "Can you please tell them Claudia?" She looked at the three Americans and said, *"Cantina Libre."*

"Do you know where that is?" Bill asked *Señor Perez*.

"Yes, I can give you the address and you can have the taxi take you there. It is about 15 minutes from here. We will call the cab for you!"

"John spoke up, "Thank you *Señor Perez* and thank you Claudia. Please don't worry. We will find them." The three of them left the office and walked outside under an overhang, safe from the drizzling rain.

Claudia left the room and started to return to her classroom, but decided she was too upset to move forward. She pulled out her cell phone and called her father, Major Nando Archuletta. She explained the entire situation she had just been made aware of, and asked him if he could help them in some way. He told her he would look into it. Her heart was heavy, and she began to pray as she walked down the hallway to her class.

****

Major Nando Archuletta, after speaking with his daughter, immediately called the Sergeant-at-Arms, who worked in the office of the General. He spoke to him rapidly and demanded to see the General-in-Command, General Miguel Agapito, of the Panamanian Army, which was actually not an attacking army, but part of the Panama Defense Forces. He was swiftly granted an audience and, after taking a short jeep ride to Head Quarters, he faced General Agapito in the small Quonset hut Command Center.

"Sir," said Major Archuletta, "There are four American girls missing, and likely kidnapped. They are young, 18-year-old teenagers who were brought down here to teach our children English. Now, we have failed to protect them, sir!"

General Agapito nodded. "I have heard of it, but have not been given the details. We will see to it, Major. I am concerned about their safety, and I do not want us to ruin our relations with the United States. Whatever you can do to help the situation would be most appreciated. You have my permission to do whatever it takes to find them. Please make it happen and see to it, Major!"

Major Archuletta stood up and snapped off a crisp salute. "Yes sir!"

****

The Cantina Libre was open for breakfast, lunch and dinner. Since it was only 11:00, it was fairly deserted, except for a few men at the bar. It had several tables and photos on the wall of many Latin military heroes from the 1800's through modern times. There were also pictures of revolutionary men and women, which explained the name *Cantina Libre*.

Bill, John and Kimmi walked in and asked for a table. They were immediately given menus, chips and salsa. When the waitress, a middle-aged woman, with dark hair and a bright smile, brought them water, they asked if they could see the owner. She smiled and said, *"Sí."*

Bill whispered, "Don't drink the water. We won't be here long anyway." The others nodded.

The waitress came back and asked them if they wanted drinks, which they declined. She said the owner would be over in a minute.

Finally, a heavy-set, mostly bald Panamanian man came over and politely asked if he could help them in Spanish.

Bill took the lead. In his best Spanish he asked about the four girls and their chaperone and told him they were missing. The owner listened and then told them that yes, they had been in a couple of nights ago, but left with their chaperone after eating dinner and having a couple of cocktails. He did not see them drive out into the night, nor did he know if they had a taxi cab.

Bill thanked him and told him they were concerned friends. He told him where the PT boat was tied up and asked him to please contact them if he heard anything.

The owner nodded, excused himself and went over to the bar to help the bartender with something to do with the cash register.

Bill waived to the waitress and told her they had to leave suddenly. He asked how much for the chips and salsa, and she told him not to worry about it. Before they left, Bill placed a five-dollar U.S note on the table for a tip.

They walked out the door and into the rain. As they left, the owner looked up and watched them leave. With his eyes squinted, he said something to the bartender, who also watched them walk out. The owner pulled out his cell phone and made a call.

As they stood there, waiting for a taxi, Bill leaned over to John and said, "That guy was lying his ass off."

John nodded. "Why did you tell him where to find us?"

Bill smiled, "You have to put out some cheese if you want to catch a rat!"

"What do we do now?" asked Kimmi.

"Head back to the boat," said Bill. No need to look for their hotel. They never left this cantina, at least under their own power. If they are alive, and I am sure they are, they were probably given something to make them pass out and then taken from here. And that S.O.B. inside knows who took them and probably where they are. I have no idea what happened to their chaperone, but he may be in on it, or possibly dead. We need to fill Manolo and Miguel in when we get back. Hopefully Jack, Charlie and Zenadia will be here soon," he finished.

Standing next to the street, he heard a voice calling from behind him. "Hey, *hombre,* you looking for those four American girls?" Then he giggled.

Bill, John and Kimmi turned around to see a bedraggled old man, dressed in little more than rags, sitting under the low overhead canopy of the Cantina, out of the rain.

Bill, Jack and Kimmi looked at each other. They walked over to within a few feet of the man, who looked to be around 60 years old, and was grinning wildly. He only had a few teeth, but he kept cackling at them.

"I seen 'em," he said in English. "I'm from the U.S. California! Woo hoo! Came here for the surfing, but wound up like this! Begging for a living. Got any money?" He cackled again.

Bill and John moved forward and stood over him, while

Kimmi stayed back and watched the road for any hostilities. Bill, the much more astute one, having been in Viet Nam and then on the Amazon Basin, said, "What do you know, old man?" He said it without kindness. He said it without malice, but he said it with force, letting the man know this was serious business and not some bullshit fairytale.

The old man cackled again. "I am Rogoman! I was the mayor of Albany and the Governor of New York! Once, I was the President of the United States! Ha ha!"

Rogoman looked up at Bill. "I seen 'em. I seen 'em carry your four girls out of the cantina and load 'em into the truck. They were cute!" He cackled again.

Bill, suddenly excited, reached down and grabbed the old man by the collar and yanked him up. "Where? Where were they taking them?"

The old man, playing the game, giggled. "How much? How much is it worth to you Bill Treese?"

Bill jumped back at the use of his name. He let go of the old man, who staggered back slightly, but was still standing. He put his hand back against the cantina wall for support. He giggled again.

"How did you…?" he began., but Rogoman was way ahead of him. "Ha, ha, I know you, Bill! I know your crew! I know I could help you retrieve the girls for the right price." He smiled.

He said, "You are looking for your friend's daughter. Ha ha! She's just meat to them. These girls are a dime a dozen. They see to the needs of the men. Then, after a few months they get rid of them. I saw her. She's pretty. Blue eyes, blonde hair. Nice body! He cackled while Bill had to hold John back from laying into the old man in his rage.

"They grabbed her first! Then the others second. She is the prize! Ha ha! They won't violate her of course. They'll give her to the military. Then General de Luna, will take her first and then sell her to one of his friends for a million bucks or more.

"Remember, the jungle on the *Rio Atrato* has eyes. It will be witness to your death! Ha ha! Anything else? I need money!"

Bill pulled out a $50 U.S. dollar bill and a $100 dollar bill. He tossed the fifty to Rogoman and held up the $100 note. He smiled, "Yours if you want it. Who took the girls?"

"You need to add four more of those if you really wanna' know! Because my life will be over now. It will be forfeit! If I tell you, then I need it to get away. Your choice! Ha ha!"

Bill looked at John, who shrugged. "OK, five hundred." Bill peeled off the bills and handed them to the old man, who took them reluctantly, as if it was his death sentence. He never looked up. "Toyota Land Cruiser Troop Carrier. 1980. It's known as a Troopie. White color, with some camouflage. No plates. They're heading for the Darién Gap. Then to Cartagena, then Bogota and down to the interior of Colombia. General de Luna wants them. Find the jeep, before it reaches the *Rio Atrato*, otherwise you will have to swim!" He cackled again, "Ha ha!"

"General de Luna acts as if he's an honorable man, but he's just interested in the money. There's another General from here who is over him and nobody knows his name. He's the real boss! He's the bad one! He has a vendetta against them girls and whoever they came down with. And on top of that, he wants the gold from the lost mines! Ya!"

"What mines?" asked Bill, "Not the *Espiritu Santo Mine at*

Cana? That played out in 1912!"

"They know something. Not that mine. Another one near Atrato River, off one tributary. The big General knows there is still gold there, but it's guarded by the Little People! Ha ha! They will kill you and keep the gold! They're the killers of the jungle. You never see them until you pass into the gold mines. The mystery General doesn't know about 'em and General de Luna doesn't care!

"So now you have two generals that are crazy! Ha ha!" Rogoman looked around quickly from side to side, as though he had already said too much, but he couldn't stop now. His voice was rising, almost against his will.

"But, de Luna, he's a pig. I know him. I was one of his soldiers. I stopped him once from doing bad things to nice girls. He knocked out my teeth! He cut off my nuts! He had me emasculated! He destroyed my life! Now you! You're here to rescue the girls he covets! You can stop him! Stop him for me. Kill him! Yes, yes! Ha ha! He acts innocent, but he really wants to violate the young girls! He wants to do bad things to them, like before. He wants to sodo-," suddenly several shots rang out from across the street and Rogoman's body was thrown back against the wall of the Cantina! He slipped down to the dirt and lay under the low overhead canopy, gasping weakly.

Bill, John and Kimmi dove out of the way, but then Bill ran back over to Rogoman. He knelt down beside him and pulled him up into his arms. Rogoman was whispering something. Bill listened intently.

"Find Maltilda," he wheezed, as his eyes stared straight ahead wildly. "He was at the mine with Jake Marley! He's 90 plus years and took the gold bar. Tell him to put it back so we can all rest in peace!"

"Where? Where?" asked Bill.

"Choco! Choco!" he cried, then his head fell back as he died. More shots rang out, and Bill ducked down below as bullet fragments shattered the stucco wall above his head. He ran to join John and Kimmiko, as they raced down the street to escape the barrage of bullets. They made it to an area, three blocks away from the cantina, and, seeing a yellow taxi just sitting there, they piled in, and told the cabbie to take them to the PT boat!

Once they arrived at the dock, Bill told Manolo and Miguel about what had happened. The rain had let up some, but the air was still heavy with moisture.

They all sat in the galley together. Manolo held Kimmi who was shaking silently and had her eyes closed. Bill, sitting next to John, asked Miguel if they had heard from Jack or Charlie. He said they had landed and were taking a taxi here to the boat, but it would take an hour.

John asked Bill, "How did that guy know your name?"

"I have no clue whatsoever," said Bill.

Kimmi looked up, firmly held by Manolo's strong arms, "Why did they have to kill him? How did they know he was telling us those things?"

John looked at his daughter. It seemed that no matter where he brought her, trouble always followed. "Honey, we don't really know," said John, "But it was likely the owner of that cantina made a phone call when we left or somehow got word to someone to watch us and make sure no one helped us. That man wasn't just looking for money, he was getting back at someone. Maybe that General de Luna he mentioned. He said he knew him. He said he ruined his life. He made it sound like no one would touch the girls until the very end – just before they're sold, he might try to have his way with one or all four of them. So, we need to get down there ASAP! When Jack gets here, we need to move out quickly. I don't know if more bad guys might show up, because Bill let them know where we were tied up," he paused, "for good reasons, of course!"

Bill smiled, "Yes, we want someone else to come here to get more information out of them! There has to be hundreds of those jeeps he mentioned. How will we find that exact one? Also, he mentioned the Rio Atrato in the Darién Gap. That is called the most dangerous jungle in the world for good reason. People come there from other countries and try to sneak into the United States. They enter there, move through Central America, through Mexico and into the U.S. Many never make it out alive. There are deadly snakes, spiders and animals that can kill you. Disease is rampant there. Many of the ones who traffic women, girls and boys, go the opposite direction, like the old man said. They move from that jungle into Colombia and spread through South America, and even the rest of the world. There are also Communist military rebels who fight the armies of Colombia and Panama. The governments of the two countries can also be drawn into the conflict. The worse thing for people down there is to get between two or more warring factions. Oh, and don't forget the drug traffickers! You have quite an unlawful mess down there!"

John was pensive, "Yes, and there is one other wrinkle.

There is a search for a lost treasure there, in the middle of the jungle. It's a mine that had a ton of gold that came out of it in the late 1800's, only to be stopped for no apparent reason, like you said, in 1912. Many people have gone there, looking for more treasure. But, according to legend, there is another gold mine near there, but close to the river. That's what Rogoman was talking about. A lost gold mine near the River Atrato. Then again, according to legend, a group went down there just after World War II, but were apparently ambushed and killed. No one really knew what happened to them. Apparently one survived, but the legend has not been spoken of, or explored for over 60 years - and good luck trying to find him down here!"

Bill said, "Rogoman said the lone survivor was named Maltilda and he still lives in the town of Choco, which is on the Atrato River. But, with all due respect, why would we care about a missing treasure when Jack's daughter's life may be at stake?"

"Good question, but apparently the bad guys are also on the trail to the lost treasure, so we need to keep that in mind," said John.

"How do you know that for sure, other than what Rogoman said?" asked Bill.

"Before we left Jamaica," said John, "I was told all about the Lost Treasure of the Darién Gap. The gold was mined down there, but even more was captured from Cortez and his bloody crew. They were pirates and invaders." said John. "There is believed to be a hundred million in gold bars hidden in that damn lost mine. No one knows how many have tried to find it since then, but rumor has it, there was that one disastrous expedition in 1946. People were killed and, according to legend, only one of the thousands of gold bars was brought out. Apparently, they were attacked by things, 'not of this earth,' which is what they said. That is why it scares the shit out of me! And there's not much on this earth that scares the shit out of me!" The others nodded.

"Yeah," said Bill, "but it didn't make sense. Rogoman said that Maltilda was at the mine with Jake Marley. That would make him 90 plus years old, I guess. He supposedly took a gold bar from the lost mine before he escaped. Rogoman said to tell him to put it back so they can all rest in peace! He said the little people would kill us and they ruled the jungle. He said they are the killers of the jungle. What the hell does all of that mean?"

Before anyone could answer, there was a knock on the top hatch, and the familiar voice of Jack Paris yelling down, "Anybody home?"

Everyone stood up at once. "Coming up Jack!" called Bill. They all took turns climbing the ladder to the deck. Bill was the first to greet Jack, with a big hug. He looked into Jack's eyes, "How are you holding up, buddy?"

Jack smiled thinly and shrugged. "Just want to find my baby and get her back home to our family." He looked away, blinking back the tears. John was the next up and then Manolo and Kimmi. They also gave Jack hugs and whispered words of encouragement to him. Last was Miguel, who didn't know Jack as long as the others had, but still embraced him and said into his ear, "We'll get her back for you, Dr. Jack!"

Jack said, "Thank you all, and for sacrificing your time and putting yourself on the line for my family!"

Bill asked, "Did Charlie fly back home?" He looked a little disappointed.

Jack smiled, "No she is paying the taxi." He looked back and pointed, "There they are now!"

They all turned to see Charlie and Zenadia walking toward the PT boat carrying heavy, camouflaged bags and backpacks.

John was excited, "Wow, cool! You did bring the whole gang, after all!"

"I couldn't have kept them away," smiled Jack.

They came up the gang plank. Charlie spoke up, "Well, Bill, I see you put this tub back together! Does she still run?" she smiled.

Bill laughed. He went to hug her and then hugged Zenadia. "I am so happy to see you both! It's going to be dangerous, but our odds of success just doubled or," he looked at Zenadia, who smiled at him, "maybe just tripled!"

Bill turned to Manolo, "Let's help them to stow their gear below." He turned to Charlie, "By the way, may I ask what you have brought onto my vessel?" It was an old joke between them from Viet Nam.

"You may ask," laughed Charlie.

"Uh, is it dangerous?"

"Yes."

"For me or the enemy?"

"Definitely for the enemy, Sir!" she snapped off a crisp salute.

Bill sighed, "Just like the old days in Nam!" He paused, "Manolo, that's OK, just stay put. I'll take the ladies down below deck."

They descended the ladder to the galley. "Zenadia, you can take Miguel's quarters. He can sleep in the forecastle."

Zenadia nodded and immediately went into Miguel's cabin, to stow her gear away.

"Charlie," he began, but she had already moved into Bill's Captain's Quarters.

"I'll sleep in here with you Bill Treese," she said. I brought a sleeping bag!" Bill started to protest that he could sleep somewhere else, but Charlie put up a hand, "Oh, please stop, Bill! You survived Viet Nam. Don't you think you can survive sharing a cabin with me? I'm too damn old to hurt you, after all!" She giggled, "You think after 35 plus years, I'm going to let an opportunity like this get away from me?" She laughed again. "Besides, we're here on business and we have a job to do. Any objections?" Bill smiled and shook his head. "No sir!" he saluted.

Just then Zenadia came out, "I would really rather sleep on deck, if that's ok, or even in that cabin you have on deck. Isn't it called a day cabin? I can put my gear in there."

"Yes," said Bill, "but it can get hot in there!"

Zenadia shot him a quick look and smiled, "Do you think I am afraid of the heat after all that we have been through? Besides, I don't sleep. I watch, and my third eye watches over all of us! The sea and the wind are still my friends. I will sleep with my eyes open!

Bill laughed at the second inside joke of the day, "Suit yourself girl," as Zenadia swung around, climbed back up the ladder and entered the day cabin.

After a while, they all assembled on deck.

Bill, started. He was in command of this mission and would not relinquish it.

'So," Bill said, "It is time to address this."

****

Jazmine Paris knew she had been kidnapped. She had no idea why and she could only hope that her parents and those she cared about were working to get her the help she needed. She felt her hands tied behind her back. She was blindfolded and pressed against someone, probably her friend Jackie, but she couldn't be sure. She felt they were moving in a vehicle, maybe a truck, somewhere, bumping along a rough road, moving ahead, but it was damp and cold. There were muffled voices around her, probably in the cab or front of the truck. They were speaking some kind of slang Spanish, or maybe the local dialect. They kept laughing, as if someone was telling them jokes that she couldn't understand. In spite of her ability to understand classic Spanish, she could only pick up about half of what was being said. She was sick to her stomach. The tranquilizing agent she had been given hadn't worn off and she felt like she was going to pass out again. Everything her parents said and feared was coming true. Now she was on some terrible truck, in a terrible jungle and about to experience some terrible fate, she could only imagine.

She started to panic and the scream that arose in her throat, was only stifled by a strong effort to harden her heart at the last moment. She took a deep breath, which calmed her down. Her survival skills had kicked in and her mind shifted into not just survival, but fight and attack mode. Her sudden anger fed her courage and she tried to think clearly.

There was a reason for this. In the 1970's, her dad, Jack Paris, had trained in his teens with many people who had studied with Bruce Lee in the San Francisco Bay Area, not long after Bruce passed away. There was an entire subculture of young people, who had trained with his disciples, that had been members of Bruce's Oakland dojo. Jack was one of them. He had mastered many difficult fight sequences and developed unique combat skills. Jack, in turn, taught his children the discipline of Jeet Kune Do, which Bruce founded in the 1960's.

Jazmine began to steel her mind against her kidnappers and mentally prepared to fight back. The weak links, however, were the other three girls. She didn't know how they would react to their situation, because they were supposed to be returning home right now. She also didn't know their kidnapper's intentions. She doubted they would go to this much trouble just to kill them. She had read enough to know they trafficked women down here and sold them into slavery. So, in that regard, she knew they had value, and, in a strange way, would be protected, at least until they were sold. Then, at that point, she realized, all bets were off. She took another deep breath and waited to see what would happen next.

CHAPTER SIX

THE DARIÉN GAP

BILL HAD ASSEMBLED EVERYONE ON DECK AT at the bridge of the PT boat. On hand were Jack, John, Kimmi, Manolo, Miguel, Charlie and Zenadia. Bill had brought everyone up to speed on the events that had transpired that day. He told them, "From everything we can tell, the girls, and maybe their chaperone, are being transported in a 'Troopie' vehicle to the Darién Gap, which is considered to be the most dangerous jungle in the world. Then it's likely they will be moved by boat, possibly down river on the Atrato River, to the Caribbean then on to Cartagena. From there, they could continue either though South America or to some Middle Eastern country. But they could wind up anywhere and that's the rub. We don't know how to track them through the jungle, but we may be able to intercept them on the river and attack their vessel. There has been talk that the people who took them are also trying to get to the gold mines of the Lost Treasure of the Darién Gap. If so, that could hold them up long enough for us to intercept them and get the girls back."

Jack spoke up, "So, we are here in Colon and are going to try to enter the Darién River at the Isthmus, where it empties into the Caribbean Ocean. Then we'll sail upriver until we get to…., where?"

Bill cleared his throat and looked away.

"What if the kidnappers and the girls are going up through Mexico, in the opposite direction?" continued Jack. "Or why don't they just go from Colon and sail to Cartagena directly and sell the girls there? Seems like an easier play than traveling through this damn dangerous jungle. Right?"

Bill spoke quietly, but firmly, as everyone listened intently. "Your right, but they don't just want the girls, they want the gold. That's the ticket!" he said looking around at all of them. "We have more than one source, which has said there are several issues going on. First, that being said, the most logical trek for the kidnappers to find the gold and sell the four girls is through the Darién Gap, then to Cartagena, through Columbia, to South America, the Middle East, or Europe. They avoid detection from the Panamanian Navy by not going directly from Colon to Cartagena, which the authorities might expect and would likely be on the lookout for them. They won't go to Mexico, because there are police and *Federales*, friends of the U.S., who would try to return the girls, for political and moral reasons. Also, the headmaster told us that Claudia, one of the Panamanian girls who became close friends with Jazmine, is the daughter of Major Nando Archuletta, of the Panamanian Army. It is entirely likely that she has alerted her dad and he may be mobilizing their forces right now to try to help the girls. It would be a big-time black eye politically, if these four young American girls were kidnapped right under their noses of people who were supposed to protect them! Plus, it was obvious from Claudia's reaction, that she was extremely upset about the disappearance and would likely ask her dad to help out. She appeared to be a very sweet and sensitive girl, who would likely want to help in any way she could. I am guessing, but it seems very likely. So, sailing on the open sea would be an easier find than traveling through a dense jungle and down a dangerous river! But they are greedy and want to find the gold, which puts them on a collision course with the jungle of the Darién Gap!

"Once they get through the jungle, which is no easy task, then they will likely be transported by boat downriver. The river is shallow in many places and could present an obstacle for us in the PT boat. If they just want to get the girls out of the jungle and sell them, they will probably exit the Atrata River at the Isthmus, where we will be entering and moving upriver. However, if they do have an interest in the gold, then they would stop at the mine Rogoman was talking about, to explore the area and search for the lost gold. Not sure how much time they are willing to spend there, or if they have made other attempts, but that is the most likely scenario. If so, they will collect what they can, then bring the girls downriver. It's important to know, the mine is reported to have a fortune in gold bars, but is guarded by what Rogoman called the 'Little People', whoever or whatever they may be. The gold was apparently mined around the same time as the *Espiritu Santo Mine at Cana.* That mine produced around four tons of gold, but this one was smaller and not as productive. When it was abandoned, the jungle eventually reclaimed it, but people continued to look for it. The most famous expedition was just after World War II, but apparently there has been no gold exploration since then that we know of."

Charlie spoke up, "What happened then?"

Bill continued, "So just after World War II, a small expedition came down here and supposedly found a way into the mine, which was a feat in and of itself, as any opening to the mine had been sealed by rock slides, mud slides, floods and jungle overgrowth. Apparently, there was only one survivor, who brought out a gold brick and a wild story about being attacked by something, he described as 'not of this earth.' Even though others have explored down there, no one has found a way in, and there have been no attacks. But, legend has it, there is over $100 million in gold bricks in there, which has never been recovered. So, our kidnappers, in addition to smuggling women, cocaine, weapons and other contraband, are looking to score some ancient gold, as well."

John said, "Tell them what that guy who died at the Cantina told you."

Bill suddenly looked uneasy. He looked around, as if someone else might be listening in on their conversation. "He said to find Matilda, some elderly man in the Choco region. He said he was on that expedition in 1946, where everyone was killed but he escaped. Somehow, that guy, Rogoman knew where to find him. He said to go to Choco, a village in the Darién Gap." He paused, "Then he said something weird. He said to tell Maltilda to put the gold bar back so they could all have some peace! I have no idea what that's about, but it may be worth exploring when we get to the Atrato River. But I don't know about that yet. It depends on what we find as we sail."

No one said anything for a minute. Finally, Jack asked, "What's so special about this jungle that makes it so uninhabitable?"

Bill smiled, "Have you ever heard of the Pan American Highway?"

Jack nodded, but was silent.

Bill said, "The Pan American Highway runs from Alaska to the tip of Argentina for about 30,000 miles, except for a 55-mile gap between Columbia and Panama. This area is called the Darién Gap. It is affectionately known as the most dangerous jungle in the world. There has been talk of building a connecting road, but the fear is it would damage the environment, and aid the smugglers who work and live down there. The jungle is surrounded by swamps, mountains, unmarked trails, drug traffickers, smugglers, Colombian guerrillas, malaria-carrying mosquitos, and no real law enforcement. Not to mention, giant killer snakes, crocodiles, caimans, deadly spiders and big killer cats. There is no food or water. It is a damn, dangerous place.

"You need a powerful, 4-wheel drive vehicle, which might not be enough and could get stuck, especially in the rainy season. If you can't get out, then sooner or later, someone will come by and either kidnap you for ransom, or just kill you outright. There aren't very many kind people in that jungle.

"So, the good news, if there is any, is that the kidnappers would be motivated to keep the girls safe, because they're worth money to them alive and unmolested. Especially if they're young and pretty, which it sounds like they are. It would help if we could find their chaperone. What was his name?"

"*Señor Roberto*," answered Jack.

"Right, so he either sold the girls out, or got sold out

himself. No one knows where he is, and that may be a problem, especially if he is in on this."

Jack began to see red and had to contain himself. He and the rest of the parents had trusted *Señor Roberto*, but now he wasn't so sure.

John said, "So what are we going to do, Bill?"

"We are going to leave here in two hours after we refuel and head south to the Isthmus of the Atrato River, then head upstream. We will need to look and listen for clues and also look for any military people who might look suspicious. Since this is a pretty lawless area, I am not really concerned about running into any legitimate *Federales*. In fact, depending on who we run into, we may have to fight to survive. We will be moving towards the Cana Valley, where the gold mine is, not to look for gold, but to look for the people who took the girls. That is our priority, first and foremost. We need a miracle. We may stop at that place, Choco, to look for Maltilda, but we can't waste any time. He may be important, or he may not be. Also, just to be on the safe side, I've taken the liberty to contact my own sources to watch the docks in Cartagena and other places they might show up. They'll alert us to anyone who might look out of place or act weird, traveling with four young girls, which would be highly unusual in these waters. Having said that, we know we can't trust anyone else down here, and that is important! Now let's get moving!"

Bill spent the next hour going over the PT boat functions, weaponry, safety features and how to pilot the boat with Charlie and Zenadia.

An hour later, after fuel, food and water had been brought on board, they cast off for the Darién Gap.

****

Señor Roberto knew he had been kidnapped. He was face down on the metal bed of some kind of truck, being bounced through rough terrain. His hands were tied behind his back, his feet were bound, and he was blindfolded. He had a gag in his mouth. For some reason, he had no idea where he was and couldn't remember where he had been. His mind was a haze. He didn't think he drank too much alcohol, because he wasn't a big drinker and never took drugs. He was hot and sweating profusely. Whatever he was riding in, was grinding its gears and shifting constantly. He felt it move uphill for a time, then back downhill. He was sick to his stomach, but tried to steel himself so he would not get sick and aspirate. Suddenly, he felt the vehicle slam to a stop, with a maniacal screeching of the brakes.

He laid still, pretending to be unconscious, as he listened to muffled voices. It wasn't clear what they were saying, other than talking about tossing something off a cliff.

With a loud crash, he heard the rear steel doors open and felt strong hands pulling him out. He landed with a painful crash onto a dirt road, and let out a loud *oooooomph!* He heard the men around him laugh and then felt someone kick him in his side. He let out a moan, but didn't move or try to protect himself. Not that he could have, anyway.

Someone rolled him over onto his back with their boot. He was breathing heavily, mostly due to fright, but also from the painfully rough ride. Someone reached down and yanked off his blindfold. The harsh glare of the sun, shining through a break in the clouds, hit him fully in the face. He yelped and closed his eyes protectively, strangling around his gag. The men surrounding him laughed, but he didn't protest or fight. He knew he was at their mercy and wanted to cooperate. He still had no idea what had happened, but his mind was beginning to come around, and he thought he remembered he was supposed to be here to protect someone. But who?

As he lay on the ground, his eyesight began to return to normal. He had a terrible headache, but he didn't know why. As he looked around, he saw the men were soldiers in camouflage garb, carrying military weapons. There were several of them and were milling around, talking, as though they were waiting for someone to arrive. He was confused. There was something wrong, but he didn't know what he had done, and he was starting to realize what they might be going to do to him.

After about five minutes in the sweltering heat, he heard a vehicle approach, which sounded like a jeep. Sure enough, an open military jeep suddenly appeared and pulled up next to the vehicle, he assumed he had been riding in. As he looked around, a military officer got out of the passenger seat and walked over toward him. He heard the loud crunch of heavy boots on the gravel road. He was still gagged and tied up, unable to move.

The officer stood over him and looked down for a few seconds. He began to speak, "So, Roberto, we meet again after all of these years!"

The voice sounded familiar, but he couldn't place it. He shook his head to indicate he didn't understand him.

The man, who wore a Supreme General's uniform knelt down and grasped Roberto by his shirt with both hands. He pulled him up violently to his feet, so they were face to face, inches apart.

"It is me, your former girlfriend Mary's cousin, Juan Velasco! But now I am Supreme General Juan Velasco! And I am in charge of all of this," he gestured by moving his chin in all directions around him, "eternal jungle and all of the dangerous beings in it!"

He continued, "The night you betrayed me at that soccer game, your Papa came to visit me to settle your affairs. But he didn't come alone to keep your honor. He was too much of a *putah!* He brought along two men who ambushed me and beat me up. Then he suggested I join the Army. So, guess what? I did! Now I am the ruler of all you see! And I am going to say goodbye to you as we cast you over the cliffs! I could tie you to a giant ant farm to eat you alive, or to a tree for the jaguars to chew your heart out, or float you into a river filled with piranha; but I want the pleasure of throwing you over the cliff and listen to you scream as you fall to your death! He shoved Roberto back onto the ground violently." Juan Velasco paused for a few seconds, looking down at him. He continued, "Don't worry about your precious little girls you have brought down here. They will be stripped and sold to the highest bidders who will make them their sex slaves for the rest of their lives, as long as they please my customers. But in the meantime, my men will have their time with them, as they too, deserve some pleasure!

"Get him up," he said to the guards. "Take off the shackles on his legs and arms, but hold him tight! Pull out his gag! I want to hear him scream while he falls into the cavern!"

The men did as they were told. Roberto, his mind racing, had come fully to his senses. He knew everything now, but the overriding issue on his mind was, that he somehow had to save the girls. He didn't know where they were, but it was one hundred percent his fault that they had been kidnapped and somehow, someway, he had to survive.

Roberto remained silent, but he steeled his heart to do his best to live. His one thought was, *I need to save the girls who trusted their lives to me. No matter what!*

The soldiers led him along the trail. He heard rushing water ahead of them. The closer they got, the louder it became. They reached the end of the trail and he saw what he feared the most; a fast-rushing river, flowing over into a waterfall which fell over 1,000 feet. The roar of the falls was overwhelming. The men stood on the bank, as they took it all in, the fast-flowing river, the dense jungle and the deep gorge which stretched out endlessly in front of them, surrounded by mountains covered in clouds and an eerie mist. The scene was surreal, as if painted by a master artist who wanted to show off the cruel beauty of the jungle falls at their most intrinsic moment, lost in time. Suddenly, Supreme General Juan Velasco, grabbed Roberto and spun him around. He slapped him hard across the face twice, drawing blood. "Now die *putah!*" he screamed as he pushed Roberto backwards off the cliff and into the falls. He disappeared into the mist, but did not scream.

Juan Velasco stood there for a moment, then spit into the river after Roberto. *Adios putah,* he thought. He then turned back to his men and gave the order to head to the rendezvous point where they would meet General de Luna, his soldiers, and the girls.

****

Jazmine Paris decided she needed to act sooner, rather

than later. The truck, or jeep, or whatever they were riding in, was bouncing over the rocks and dirt of the jungle road. She pressed against what felt like one of the other girls, who she knew she was with.

She thought it was Jackie, but it was actually Gwedolyn. She was crying quietly. Gwen knew what had happened and was feeling that she was going to be sold into slavery. She thought she would never be able to see her family again. Jazmine whispered, "Gwendolyn, are you OK?"

"No," she said, "we are being kidnapped and are not going to ever be with our families again!" Her voice started to rise, "Who is going to help us now?!"

"Quiet! Don't be afraid!" whispered, Jazmine. "We will help you."

Jackie, lying on the other side of Jazmine, began to wake up and was in shock and fearful. "What do we need to do to get away from these people?" she asked Jazmine.

Jazmine whispered, "We need to be ready for anything. We have resources. We have each other."

"Fucking A, right!" Whispered Cazzy." She was the tough one, who spoke fluent Spanish. She was lying in front of them and continued, speaking quietly, as the other girls moved closer. "Whoever these people are, they know we are worth more money untouched and undamaged. I've read about situations like this. They want the money, because we are all young and pretty. Just play along and don't panic. Don't say a lot."

Jazmine said quietly, "We've probably been driving for a while, but I have no idea how far we are from the town we were taken from, or which direction we are heading. Are you all blindfolded and have your hands tied behind your backs?"

"Yes," they all whispered.

"So am I," replied Jazmine, "I also want to know what happened to *Señor Roberto*, and was he in on this?"

The others agreed quietly. They all braced themselves for what was going to happen next.

****

Bill had been driving the PT boat all afternoon and even through the dinner break. Manolo, to the delight of Charlie and Zenadia, had made a special dish called *Bandeja Paisa*, the national dish of his home in Colombia. It was made of rice, avocado, minced meat, chorizo, fried pork rind, sausage, corn cakes and topped with fried eggs. It was a calorie dense meal intended to satisfy the greatest hunger, which it did. Manolo had also included several colas, which he had procured on their last visit to the mainland. Even though Bill, John, Miguel and Kimmi were used to Manolo's great food, they were none the less, always grateful for it. It was followed up by hot Chocolate con Queso, which was a dessert of cheese dipped in hot chocolate. The hot chocolate and the stringy melted cheese, made a good combination. They all drank and ate it up enthusiastically.

Only Jack picked at his food, his mind on his daughter Jazmine and what she might be facing at this very minute. He knew he had to eat to keep up his strength, because he would need it to survive and to fight. But he was running on adrenaline and could not eat or sleep. He could only focus on the mission at hand.

Miguel came up on deck to give Bill a break so he could

eat. Bill showed Miguel the coordinates on the map and also on the radar he was tracking. They would hit the Atrato River Isthmus in about one hour. The water was fairly deep and easy to navigate for a while, but eventually, they might bottom out, in spite of the relatively shallow draft of the PT boat.

Bill went below and joined everyone in the galley. He ate the excellent food Manolo had prepared, and drank two of the cokes. There would not be any drinking of alcohol on board for the foreseeable future, because they all knew there were four young girls, whose lives were at stake, and they could not afford to get sloppy. Bill ate quickly and was about to go back to the Bridge, when he spotted Jack, sitting away from the others looking down sadly.

"Hey Jack," Bill called to him, "can you spare a minute?"

Jack looked up and nodded.

Bill started for his cabin and motioned for Jack to come with him. Once inside, Bill closed the hatch for privacy. He sat on his bunk and told Jack to sit in his Sea Captain's chair. Jack sat down.

Bill was not going to mince words. "Jack, you know this is life and death."

Jack nodded.

Bill continued, "I have no doubt you and Lisa warned your daughter about making this trip, but here we are. I want you to know, the odds are on our side. I am 99.9% certain we have the correct info on where they are going to be taken. These drug runners and kidnappers are not the sharpest tools in the shed. They are generally a greedy lot, who act, but don't think. I've dealt with them for years on the Amazon. Your girls are pretty.

They are young and they are, please forgive me, very desirable to the bad people of the world. They will be kept alive, unharmed and unmolested until they can be sold. We are going to intercept them before that happens. But, I want to be clear, and you and I have been through a lot down here - it is kill or be killed. When you shoot…shoot to kill. Be safe. Protect yourself and the man or woman next to you, but don't take any prisoners. They have already forfeited their lives because of what they are doing. Don't forget that!"

Jack nodded again.

"We have everything we need right here; Charlie, with her CIA and Viet Nam experience, us with our guns, and you know what Zenadia is capable of. We will get your girls back to you! Any questions?"

Jack, still looking down, shook his head.

"OK. We will enter the Atrato River in about an hour. Get some sleep if you can, because we'll reach our first port in about six hours and I need all hands-on deck then."

Jack got up without saying anything and went to the forecastle to try to get some sleep.

Bill watched him leave. *Well, that went well,* he thought sarcastically. He left his cabin and went up to the Bridge to check in with Miguel.

****

The truck Jazmine, Gwendolyn, Jackie and Cazzy were riding in came to a sudden stop with a loud screech of brakes, sounding like metal on metal. The girls were all awake and on alert. They heard the men piling out and moving towards them. It was cold and wet, with a light rain falling. Their back door flew open, and the men dragged the girls out into the rain and onto the wet dirt road, where they shoved them down into the mud. In spite of themselves, the girls screamed, and began to yell for help.

The soldiers stepped back and began to laugh out loud at them. Another jeep with a canvas cover came up and General Xavier De Luna stepped out. He strode over to the four American girls and removed their blindfolds. They could see very little, as it was late at night and the rain was starting to come down harder. Overhead, the clouds moved quickly and a strong wind began to blow.

General de Luna told the girls to stand up. He was brutal and they knew it. "What do you young ladies need?" he asked in English. "Food? Water? Do you need to pee?"

Jazmine, the chosen leader said, "Yes, sir. All of the above. But can we please have a little privacy, sir?"

The General smiled and snorted. He turned to his lieutenant and said in Spanish, "Take them one at a time into the jungle and let them relieve themselves. Let them move a few feet in front of you and give them some privacy, for the love of God. But remember to keep their shackles on. Then when you bring them back, you can feed them." The soldiers snickered, thinking lewd thoughts.

The General turned to the girls. "One at a time," he said in English. "No tricks and no trying to escape. There are many things out there that would like to eat you and you will die very quickly in this jungle if you try to leave us." The girls all shivered with his words, which chilled them to their bones. He smiled,

"Now, who wants to go first?"

Gwendolyn nodded her head, "Please sir. I need to go badly."

The General motioned to his lieutenant and the process began.

Once the girls had returned from the jungle, they were all given water and some crackers, plus some tins of greasy sardines, but were never relieved of their bindings. The soldiers had to hand-feed them their food. The girls all noticed the soldiers were filthy and they stank of sweat, urine and the smells of the jungle. Because they were starving, they ignored the health risk posed by the guards and ate anyway, never looking their captors in the face. Then they were shuttled back into the jeep and were driven off into the night.

CHAPTER SEVEN

THE RIVER ATRATO

THE PT BOAT HIT THE ISTHMUS OF THE Atrato River in one hour, as planned. Bill made the necessary calculations and turned his boat upriver and into the current. He navigated the obstacles which came at him quickly including logs, trees, sediment and dirt. He was sailing slowly and looking in every direction for any boat that looked like a military vessel. He continued to move up stream. The Atrato River was wide, but not nearly as wide as the Amazon River, where he felt at home. Bill throttled forward. The water was deep here and would support his boat. He knew it would eventually play out upstream, but he hoped they would make their quest before it became too shallow to support the PT boat. He planned to stop for fuel about 80 miles upriver at a town called Riosucio. He had been given the name of a man there that could sell him the gasoline he needed. After that, he didn't know where he could get more gas, so he just had to hope the extra fuel tanks he had installed a couple of years ago would be enough. Bill was going to be at the helm all night. He couldn't have slept if he had tried anyway. He was too amped up and had shifted himself into overdrive to find Jazmine and the girls. Nothing else mattered to him. He had decided their young lives were worth more than his life, which was what propelled soldiers on the battlefield to move forward, sometimes one inch at a time.

The night before, since leaving the town of Colon, the soldiers and the girls had traveled on a rough, but paved road all the way to the town of Yaviza, which was basically the end of the civilized trail. Then they turned and headed southeast into the jungle on a wet, bumpy road. After their stop for rest and food, they had traveled all the way to the Atrato River, far from where it emptied into the sea, but further upriver from the reported lost gold mine. Finally, their jeep came to an abrupt halt.

Once again, the soldiers came back and grabbed them out of the bed of the truck, forcing them to the ground. They were led, single file, to a river. It was still dark, and the rain was following and picking up speed. There was a boat there and General de Luna appeared and told the girls to get aboard, which they did. They were told to go to the stern, or the rear of the boat and lie down. The soldiers put a heavy canvas tarp over them. They were told in Spanish it was to protect them from the rain, but each one of them knew it was so they would not be seen by the *Federales*, if there were any in this lawless jungle. They were still shackled, so they lay on their sides as best they could. They only had their hands tied behind their back, but no more blindfolds. It was almost as if the soldiers knew there would be no turning back for the girls and no hope going forward. Together, the soldiers each hoped they could take turns with the young girls, but they knew they would be shot dead if they did.

The girls felt the boat move out. It seemed reasonably large, maybe 50-60 feet, but they didn't know because of the darkness. The engines were fairly quiet, but they could feel the hum of the motors through the deck of the boat. The vibrations soothed their already exhausted minds and, in spite of their intense fear, they all slipped off into a deep sleep.

General Xavier De Luna was at the helm of this patrol boat. He was heading down the Atrato River, towards the Isthmus, which emptied into the Gulf of Darién and then to the Caribbean Ocean. They were going to travel to a spot near Cartagena, Colombia where the girls would be processed and then sold. But before that, he intended to stop and look for a gold mine he had been told about, near a tributary off the Atrato River. There was a legend he had researched, about an expedition after World War II, that had found gold, only to lose the treasure and never be seen alive again. There may have been one survivor, but he was probably dead after 70 years. He looked back at the girls sleeping under the canvas tarp. They wouldn't be any trouble. With nowhere to turn, they would stay on the boat with one or two of his men. After they did some exploring, they would travel down the river and meet up with Supreme General Juan Velasco, and make some decisions about the girls and who their next victims would be. If he found gold, he would share it with General Velasco, who had actually told him earlier about the mine and the possible location in the first place. Then they would bring in more men to take out the gold, or mine it, depending on what state they found it in. He smiled. *The girls would so much need their sleep once they were sold into slavery,* he thought and chuckled silently. These young American sluts thought they were so above everyone else in the world. He would show them who was the real master!

****

Dawn was breaking over the jungle. It was, in spite of the early hour, 100% humidity and already hot. As Bill Treese piloted his boat around another partially submerged log, he took a long look down river. He had driven all night, with both Manolo and Miguel taking turns on deck with him, scanning the water, looking for suspicious vessels, which could have the missing girls aboard. The full moon was out and had flooded the area in light. They didn't see one boat on the Atrato River, either heading the same direction they were going or the opposite way. They kept the boat going slowly, using their mufflers to keep the motor noise of the PT boat down, so as not to draw attention to themselves. Because, it wasn't every day you saw a World War II PT boat traveling up a river, deep in a Panamanian jungle. It obviously took them much longer to move upriver, but this was planned. The Atrato River was only 417 miles long and beyond the city of *Quibdo,* it was shallow and probably would not support the PT boat. But *Quibdo,* which was founded in 1654 as *San Francisco de Quibdo,* was the capital of the *Choco's* region. Bill knew he had been told the man Maltilda was in Choco, but he didn't know if he would or could make it that far upriver. He had also learned that there were gold and platinum mines nearby, which made it all the more important to the people who might be holding the girl's hostage. He figured the rumored gold mine was off a tributary to the Atrato River, somewhere between where they were and *Quibdo.*

They were getting close to their first stop at *Riosucio,* where he would meet a man named Alto Pelota, on the docks to buy gasoline. Looking at his gauges, he was only down 1/3 of his fuel capacity, as they had filled up in Colon, but he wanted to "top it off," because he had no idea when he might find more fuel down here.

It was 0725 and they had just moved around a bend in the river. Manolo came up on deck then with a thermos of hot, black coffee and three, foil-wrapped breakfast burritos, made of eggs, bacon, cheese and, in spite of Bill's protests to the contrary, just a few chili peppers. Plus, Manolo's hot sauce, was really only medium hot, and he knew that Bill could handle it. Manolo and Miguel ate the Madame Jeanette peppers straight up, which were some of the hottest peppers in South America and were rumored to have gotten their name after a famous Brazilian prostitute!

Bill smiled gratefully at his mate Manolo. "Thanks Manolo! I had almost given up on you!" He unwrapped one of the burritos and sniffed at it suspiciously. "Hot peppers?" he asked disappointed.

"*Capitain,* you said you needed a wake-up after driving the boat all night. This is it! Besides, there are only a few!"

"OK, OK!" Bill laughed, "No doubt they will be delicious!"

Manolo smiled and, going through the hatch in the front console, started down the ladder to return to the galley.

Bill had just polished off the second burrito and his third cup of coffee when he saw the village come into view. He came to a dead stop in the river to survey the town. Suddenly, he felt, rather than heard Zenedia behind him. She had come out of the Day Cabin, where she had been sleeping, to the Bridge, and was looking toward the village. She was dressed in a wraparound jungle-print skirt and a tight black tank top.

"Good morning," said Bill. Zenadia didn't say anything. She was looking intently at the village and the docks approximately one half-mile away.

"When you see your friend at the docks, ask him about the man Maltilda. He knows him," she said.

Bill whipped his head around, "Wait, how the hell do you know that?" he asked.

Zenadia shrugged and, without a word, went below to get food from the galley.

Bill shook his head. *Unbelievable,* he thought.

The rest of Bill's crew were at the galley table, eating the breakfast burritos. Even Jack, although he had slept badly, ate two of them and knocked back two cups of Manolo's excellent Columbian coffee. He needed the fuel. Kimmi came up and sat down next to him.

"You OK, Uncle Jack?" she asked, concern written all over her face.

"Yes, honey. Thanks for asking. But the truth is, I'm going to be wearing my war face soon and from now on. Maybe my death face. I don't know." He turned to face her and grabbed both her shoulders with his hands. He looked into her eyes and squeezed her tightly. "Just remember, Kimmi, if I am a complete asshole and if I say something nasty to you, I don't mean it! I am focused on my daughter and that's all I can really think about. But I love you and I want to thank you for being here!"

Kimmi reached over and hugged her Uncle Jack tightly. "We're going to save her, Uncle. We're going to save them all!" She pulled back to wipe a tear from her eye. Jack also pulled away before he started crying too. His heart hardened and he stood up suddenly. He climbed the ladder to see Bill on the bridge, leaving a stunned, but not too surprised, Kimmi at the table thinking how she was ready to do anything to get the girls back.

Jack appeared on the bridge. He looked towards the front of the boat and saw the village. Bill was approaching slowly, still with the engines muffled.

Jack, in spite of his anger and feelings of being one step too late, said to Bill, "Why are we going so slow? We need to hurry up and get there!"

Bill looked over at Jack. He chose his words carefully. "Yeah, we will, but I don't want to fire up the engines, because that will only draw attention to us, and we want to avoid that. I was told the guy we are going to meet will get there at 0900, which is still 15 minutes from now. So, we're good. Did you manage any sleep?"

"A little," admitted Jack.

"OK, then you can man that port machinegun. Just stand in the tub. Don't put your hands on the weapon. Put on a helmet. No life vest because it is hot. You are my guard when we hit the docks. Miguel will be up to stay at the helm, when I meet with my contact. Charlie, Kimmi and Zenadia will stay below deck so they cannot be identified. We don't want anyone to know there are females aboard or it could set us up as a target. Lots of slave traders down here. John will come up and be on the starboard machinegun. Manolo will be on the Oerlikon Cannon in the stern. Let's be casual about this. We're getting gas and then going upriver to do a little fishing."

"Right," Jack added, "In a fully armed PT boat. Shoot the fish with the torpedoes!"

"Depth charges work better," said Bill and they both laughed. Jack needed that.

The boat approached the docks, and Bill kept the idle going. John, Miguel and Manolo came up on deck. John jumped onto the starboard machine gun tub. Once Bill reached the pier, both Miguel and Manolo jumped onto the dock and began to tie up the PT boat, while Bill throttled down and shut the engines off. The sudden silence was shocking. They could hear the town beyond where they could see. They heard traffic, honking vehicles, screeching birds flying around, and the sounds of shallow river boats suddenly moving up and down the river. Jack was keeping a sharp eye out for anything that looked big enough to transport four high school girls, but there was nothing-at least not yet.

After a few minutes, a small, dark man approached the PT boat. He looked to be in his late 70's, but it was hard to tell. He was dressed in dark stained blue jeans and an oily white tee shirt. His head was covered with a faded New York Yankees baseball cap. Bill came down from the bridge. Manolo had dropped the gangplank, and Bill walked down and greeted the man before him.

Bill spoke first, "*Señor Alto Pelota*, we are hoping to buy some gasoline from you."

Señor Pelota smiled, revealing crooked, but white teeth. *Si, señor,* it is my pleasure!"

He whistled and two young men, in their late teens, approached. In rapid Spanish, he told them what to do to fill up the PT boat with high octane gasoline. Once the fuel lines were in place, Bill asked *Señor Pelota* to speak with him. They moved away from the boat to the far end of the dock.

"*Señor Pelota,*" Bill began in his best Spanish, "I don't know where to begin, but I want to know if you know anything about a failed attempt to bring gold out of a gold mine around 1946. There is a man somewhere around here named Maltilda, I wish to speak with, but I don't know where he is."

Señor Pelota was listening and nodding. He said, "Maltilda is a friend of mine. He is here, but very old. What is it you want with him?"

"We are friends of a man in Colon, who was apparently in the Army with him. He was killed and gave us a message to give to his friend Maltilda."

Señor Pelota smiled and said, "Tell me the message and I will deliver it to him."

Bill smiled and shook his head. "That I cannot do. I am sorry, but I am sworn to secrecy. Please understand, I mean him no harm, just to deliver the message from his friend."

Señor Pelota nodded, "If you wish to speak to him, I will allow one of my boys here to take you there."

"Thank you. That would be perfect. I was told he was in the Choco region."

"He was," came the reply. Bill said nothing else.

Once the PT boat was loaded with fuel, Bill was directed

to a car, which was driven by *Señor Pelota's* nephew. It was an old, 1973 Pinto, the kind that blew up because of the poor design of the rear end and the vulnerable gas tanks. This one was battered, but serviceable, and without air conditioning. The nephew had all the windows opened because of the heat and the humidity. He drove fast and got them into town, where they pulled up to a ramshackle old dwelling. Bill was surprised and asked the driver/nephew if this was the right house. He was assured it was and got out of the car. He moved towards the front porch and knocked on the screen door. There was a young girl inside, who came out. She was about 4 feet tall, had long, dark hair, and appeared lithe and athletic. She smiled wide, showing even white teeth, and looked to be no more than 13 years old. She spoke perfect English. "Ah, you have come to see my great-grandfather," she said, "He is expecting you."

"Yes," said Bill, assuming *Señor Pelota* had called ahead, "I guess so. Is he here? Mr. Maltilda?"

"Yes, and he can hear you. He is over 90, but is very strong. He is our family favorite!"

"Can I speak with him, please?" Bill was getting tired and a little cranky. *Mostly feeding off Jack with his anger and frustration*, he thought.

"I am Brianna," she said opening the screen door. "He is out back on the back porch. I will show you."

Bill followed her through the house, which, in spite of the outward appearance, was very neat and clean inside. As Bill followed her, he noticed she was small, but moved lightly on her feet, like a dancer. She wore black leotards and a tight black workout top, *probably exercising*, Bill thought. As they walked through the kitchen, they reached another screen door, which looked out into a backyard, as if it had been hacked out of the surrounding jungle. As they passed through the door, Brianna stopped and pointed to a man sitting in a rocking chair at the end of the porch. He was staring straight out at the jungle, rocking slowly.

"Papa," she called out in Spanish, "The man is here to see you now!"

Without looking up, the man in the rocking chair nodded. Bill walked over to him, while Brianna disappeared back into the house.

There was no place for Bill to sit, so he knelt slowly in front of the elderly man. He put out his hand. "Sir," he said in his best Spanish, "I am Bill Treese. I am here on a rather awkward mission. I was told your name is Maltilda, and you survived a hunt for a gold mine in 1946. Actually, you were the only survivor."

The man looked deep into Bill's eyes. He took Bill's outstretched hand, graciously and shook it firmly. His voice was strong, and in spite of his years, sitting in the rocking chair, his body looked very strong as well. "Who told you about me and why have you come?"

Bill relayed his story about the kidnapped girls and what had happened at the Cantina in Colon. "The man was named Rogoman and they shot him."

Even before Bill was finished speaking, Maltilda was nodding his head. He spoke softly, "Ahh, Rogoman! He was my friend for many years, although much younger than me. He fell onto hard times after he met the General. I told him not to join them, but he was young and brash. He was from your California, and wanted the excitement. Looking for high adventure in a foreign country, I guess." He shrugged as though it had been a useless gesture on his part. "I told him to stick to surfing, but he wanted to be a soldier and to look for gold. So sad…" his voice trailed off and he looked past Bill into the jungle as though searching back to happier times.

Bill wanted to say something, but didn't quite know how to do it. *"Señor Maltilda,* I don't quite know how to say this, but," he struggled with his Spanish, *"Como se dice,"* he said in English, "Rogoman said 'to put the gold back so you can all rest in peace'." Bill returned to speaking Spanish, "What did he mean by that."

In perfect English, Maltilda said, "That one gold bar has been a curse on us since we took it out, but I have no way to put it back. I can give it to you, but then you will be cursed as we are!"

Bill, shocked at Maltilda's ability to speak English, thought back to the Jamaican Pirate. He smiled and looked around, "It wouldn't be the first time, *amigo!" he said.*

Maltilda nodded, "Do you want it, then?" he asked.

"Will it help you?" Bill asked.

"Sí," came Maltilda's reply.

Bill sighed, "Yes, but you need to tell me where the mine is and about the 'Little People', because, if you are right, the four kidnapped girls will be there with the General and his men. That's where we will find them, at least that is the most logical place, because they will want to stop and spend time there. Hopefully, if that is the case, we can ambush them and get our girls back."

Maltilda got out of his rocking chair, without any trouble, or hesitation, and moved quickly into the house. "Wait here," he said.

Bill stood up, took in a deep breath and waited. He looked around at the surrounding jungle in the back, so close to him, and thought about how every jungle he faced came with its own set of dangers. He sighed heavily. After a minute, Maltilda returned, holding something in a greasy brown rag. He started to hand it to Bill, but hesitated. He opened the rag slowly, revealing what looked like an ordinary brick, but with the corners rounded from wear, plus it was bright yellow and looked like pure 24 karat gold. He looked into Bill's eyes for several seconds. He said in English, "If you take this, the curse will be on you and no longer on me. Are you sure you want to do this?"

Bill, being a very practical man, hesitated, but only for a second, "First tell me where the Lost Mine is located and tell me everything you know about the 'Little People' there, who guard the treasure. This may be a bargaining chip for my life, and those I hope to save."

Maltilda sat down in his rocking chair. He called back through the screen door in Spanish, "Brianna, please bring this man a chair, honey."

A minute later, Brianna brought out a cheap, folding metal chair. She placed it next to Bill, who thanked her and sat down. She hurried back into the house. Maltilda had rewrapped the brick and placed it on his lap. "Now, I will tell you everything," he said.

One hour later, Bill was carrying the wrapped brick through the living room and was about to exit. Brianna came up behind him and tapped him on the shoulder. Bill turned around and Brianna placed her small hands, on Bill's big forearm. She stood on her toes and, as Bill turned his head to the side, she kissed him lightly on the cheek. Surprised, Bill looked into her pretty brown eyes. "Bless you," she said quietly, *"Via con Dios."*

Bill nodded, "Thank you Brianna. I hope he finds peace."

She nodded, "He will now, and so will we." She looked back behind her, through the living room and back to the kitchen. They both saw Maltilda standing at the back screen door waving and smiling at them. She continued, "I pray that you will as well, my friend. I will light a candle for you and your friends!"

"Thank you, and goodbye sweetie," Bill said, "I hope to see you both again." And with that he walked to the Pinto and got inside, the late morning heat and humidity already overwhelming him.

****

Supreme General Juan Velasco's jeep was crashing through the jungle on what was supposed to be a road. He was riding in the passenger seat, and the soldier driving him, was doing his best to stay on the road, in spite of the rain and the mud they were going through. The driver, Lieutenant Gonsalves, looked in his rear-view mirror hoping to see the rest of their troops driving behind them in the Toyota Land Cruiser. There were six soldiers, plus he and the Supreme General. He could see the troop carrier behind them, skidding and trying to keep up.

Suddenly, they hit a deep rut in the road and started to slide sideways, but Lieutenant Gonsalves, turning into the skid, maneuvered expertly and kept them from rolling over. General Velasco, hanging on for dear life said, "Nice work, Jeffee, I will remember it."

Jeffee Gonsalves nodded and gripped the wheel, staring straight ahead, as though the devil himself was chasing them.

Juan Velasco had a plan. He knew from documents he had obtained, approximately where the lost gold mine was and he was heading for the Atrato river, which would lead them to the tributary, where the mine was located. At least, that's where he thought it was, given the intelligence at hand. The original plan was for his underling, General de Luna, who was in the command boat and had the kidnapped girls onboard, to go to the mine first and then report what he found to Velasco. But he was able to dispose of his enemy quicker than expected. The jungle cliff and falls were up a tributary river, not as far upstream as they had estimated, so he had made the decision that he wanted to see the mine first hand. It wasn't that he didn't trust de Luna and his men, but de Luna was, after all, a Communist, and might feel his loyalty was more to the politburo of the various countries he represented, rather than to his commanding officer. This Velasco could not allow, and he might be forced to liquidate de Luna and his men if necessary.

He smiled. There could be no room for treachery, unless it was his doing. He thought about *Señor Roberto*. He had waited many years for that moment. In his mind, he had fantasized a thousand ways to seek his revenge and kill him. That is what spurred him on from existing as a grunt soldier in the Panamanian Army to eventually become an officer. He knew as a grunt, he would never be able to find Roberto, as he had migrated to the United States and become a teacher. Because of his intelligence, ambition and contacts, he had advanced rapidly through the ranks, sometimes being promoted over the heads of others, who had more time in the Service. He always had a plan and became an expert leader of his troops. His intelligence and combat tactics at the War Games were legendary. He had also brought down many drug Kingpins, which pleased his superiors, who were, after all, trying to preserve the dignity of their country and Panamanian heritage. Of course, Supreme General Velasco knew of these drug lords because of his own drug dealing past. He knew where to find them, knew their families, suppliers and contacts, then betrayed them and brought them down. He, of course never did the dirty work himself, because he knew he might be identified. So, he simply gave orders and his men carried out the raids to the delight of the politicians of his country.

This also put him in a position to keep an eye on Roberto. He had intelligence sources in the United States, who were sworn to secrecy, under the guise, that Roberto, once a hero to the nation because of his soccer skills, had turned traitor to Panama and had to be watched for doing clandestine drug deals. It was all false, of course, but Velasco didn't care. He would never forget that day Roberto betrayed him by winning the soccer match and his father's two friends who beat him within an inch of his life. As he had often heard, and believed, revenge was a dish best served cold. Right now, Roberto was at the bottom of the falls and was very cold indeed! He chuckled to himself.

****

General Xavier De Luna was at the helm of his combat vessel. He was heading west on the Atrato River, towards the Isthmus, which would eventually empty into the *Golfo de Uraba,* or the Gulf of Darién. Well before that, they would head up a tributary river, which would lead to the Lost Gold Mine. His plan was to explore it, a take out the gold and then report to his commander, Supreme General Juan Velasco. But now there was a change of plans. General Velasco wanted to board his vessel and take command of the mission. He also wanted to see the young girls they had kidnapped, and help decide what to do with them. Velasco believed he could sell them for more money and would likely keep the majority of the profits. De Luna knew this would anger his Communist leaders, some of whom, would like to take the girls for themselves, before selling them to their colleagues. General de Luna knew he had to tread lightly and carefully. He was between a rock and a hard place. If they found the gold, Velasco, being a greedy bastard, would try to use his influence to keep most of it and give the rest to the crooked politicians to buy their favor. Then, he would turn around and sell the girls for more profits, leaving de Luna and his superiors in the lurch. He shrugged, and thought, *Oh, well, accidents happen in desperate situations. It would not be the first time a senior officer was killed in an accident by friendly fire.* He continued to monitor the water ahead, looking for any possible hostilities. There was a small military outpost where he was supposed to meet Supreme General Velasco at. He would pick him and his men up, and then proceed to the mine.

He called to his deck officer, who came over immediately and saluted him. "See to the needs of the girls," he said, "They need to be fed and also take them below one at a time to use the bathroom. You can take their bindings off so they can clean themselves properly. There is nowhere for them to go anyway." The officer saluted again and hurried back to the stern of the vessel, where the girls had been sleeping, to do what the General had asked.

****

The PT boat had left the town of *Riosucio,* and was driving upriver. Once underway, Bill had gone below for a quick nap. Miguel was at the helm. It was early afternoon, and he was driving the boat at about 20 knots, which was faster than Bill had been going that morning, but less than one half the speed the PT boat was capable of. Jack and John were in the galley, pouring over charts and maps of the region. When Bill came back to the boat, he had told them all what Maltilda had said about the location of the mine, the gold and the "Little People" who were supposedly guarding the treasure, at least back in 1946. Manolo and Kimmi were on the machine guns while Charlie and Zenadia were back with the Oerlikon Cannon, checking the firing mechanism and testing it for movement, up and down, back and forth.

Bill, having slept for two hours, woke up and, feeling refreshed, came out of his sea cabin and walked the few feet to the galley table. He joined John and Jack and looked over the map. No one was saying anything. Finally, John broke the ice. He pointed to a tributary of the Atrado river. "As an archaeologist, it looks like there could be something here," he said, pointing to a spot a few miles upriver from them.

Bill nodded, "The *Espiritu Santo Mine at Cana,* was located here," he said pointing to the map, "Near the town of Santa Cruz de Cana. Now it is pretty much buried under the jungle canopy. It was mined until 1728 by the Spanish and was then abandoned.

Almost two centuries later, the British opened it and eventually mined over 4 tons of gold. There are abandoned locomotives and other railroad equipment there, rusting in the jungle. Our spot is here," Bill said pointing to a spot on the map, which was near the Atrato River, but up the tributary which they were approaching. "The bad thing is, there are some splits in the tributary," continued Bill, "which may lead us away from the likely spot we are looking for. Also, we don't know how shallow these upstream waters are. We could bottom out, and might have to find another way in." Jack and John both nodded.

Jack said, "How will we know when we need to approach the mine?"

Bill said, "When we get close, we need to stay back and wait to see the bad guys. They are likely on a shallow bottomed military boat of some kind. They will be armed, but I don't know what kind of weapons they will have. We obviously don't want to attack the wrong boat, or it could get messy, but there won't be many crafts like that in these waters. They might be flying a National Flag, or maybe not. I think our timing is good, because the time it would take to drive from Colon to the highway, and then through the jungle, is about what it took for us to get here, driving as slow as I was." He looked over at Jack, who earlier had asked him to speed up and smiled. "Everything I do, Jack, has a reason behind it." Jack nodded and looked down. He smiled shamefacedly, but without apologizing.

John spoke up, "It would be nice if we had some aerial recon photos over this area."

Bill nodded, "Yes, but we would probably just see more of the jungle canopy, and not likely much of the river; and probably nothing that would lead us to the Lost Mine."

They were silent for a minute. "One thing that intrigues me though," said John, "In all my years in archaeology, I have never seen two separate gold mines this close together, but with nothing in between. The gold is supposed to move off the 'Mother Load', down the river and be scattered around. But this looks like there is one mine, which played out, then another completely separate mine, which is close by, but nothing in between. Anyone ever seen or heard of that?"

Bill and Jack shook their heads. "Why does it matter?" asked Jack, suddenly irritated, feeling they were losing focus on the missing girls.

John said, "Because we want to make sure we are in the right place at the right time, not off on some wild goose-chase, letting the bad guys get away with the gold and our girls." He hesitated and added, "The gold is insignificant. We want the girls back. But the gold may be the fly paper that holds them up long enough for us to get them back!"

"Say," said Bill, "Let's ask Kimmi, Charlie and Zenadia. They might have some insight. Zenadia told me that the old man was in that village back there. I was going to look for him upriver, but boom, there he was just like she said!"

Jack went up on deck and asked Kimmi, Charlie and Zenadia if they would come below and help them with a problem they were having. The ladies came down and stood around the map in the tight galley below. It was hot and they were all sweating profusely. But their discomfort was insignificant, as they all thought about the danger the missing girls were likely in. Bill and John gave them the short version of what they had figured out so far.

Kimmi was the first to speak, being the newly graduated archaeologist, "It looks to me, like the jungle has its secrets. But we know that gold is found in lodes and or veins. It exists in earth's crust, and forms when heated fluids pass through rocks which contain gold ore, and deposit it in the earth's crust."

Charlie chimed in, "The gold is heavy and moves down the streams to deposit throughout the various rivers and streams, but it seems to be absent here. The jungle is not supporting the deposit of gold downstream."

Zenadia, once again, had the best comment, "We know that there are fractures in the Earth's crust, like Kimmi said, and mountains rise, allowing hydrothermal liquids to rise into those areas and form gold-bearing quartz deposits. It seems there are two different mountain ranges, a few miles apart, but with much of the same features between the two. That being said, there is no reason to look for a 'Mother Load', which might be leaking gold tailings downriver. If we have the location of the first mine, the *Espiritu Santo Mine at Cana,* and now the second mine, which is our target, it makes sense to camp out there, because there is nothing in between."

Everyone was quiet for a minute. Bill took a deep breath. "Thank you everyone for your help. We will continue upriver as planned, and then stop near the tributary, which would lead to the lost mine. We will continue to watch for the enemy boat to come to us. As the situation arises, we will evaluate and attack, covertly, if possible, violently if necessary."

They all nodded their heads. Bill continued, "You may all return to your posts. We will eat at 1900 and then turn in. Standard watches will be held all night. We will be at the tributary at 0700, just before dawn. I need everyone on deck at 0600. Things could get very hot, very fast. And I'm not talking about the weather out here. Can someone send Manolo down here please?"

Everyone moved out, while Bill, Jack and John tarried over the maps, making final plans for their attack and defense. Jack decided he needed to ask the question no one was asking, "Bill, you said we have to be careful not to attack the wrong boat, but if the girls are on the boat we identify, then how can we attack them? We can't fire at them, because we can't risk the safety of the girls."

Bill said, "Unfortunately you are right, Jack. We absolutely cannot use the firepower of the PT boat, because of the civilian girls on board." He sighed.

After a few minutes, Manolo came down. "Yes *Capitain* Bill?" he asked. Without looking up, Bill asked, "Can you make something simple for dinner that we can have leftovers for breakfast in the morning? I want this to be simple and fast. We are in a crunch for time."

"Uh, *Si*, I could make hash!"

They all turned to him and laughed. Bill grimaced and said, "Maybe something a little better?"

"*Si, Capitain*, I will work on it."

Two hours later, Manolo did not disappoint anyone. He called out to Bill at the helm that supper was served. Everyone came down except Bill, who stayed on deck to navigate the boat. Miguel offered to drive, but Bill wanted to stay a little longer.

They all came down to the crowded galley. Manolo set out a huge pot of *sancochos*, a stew of a combination of chicken, pork and beef, simmered and cooked for a long time, (actually since last night, as he had anticipated this scenario). He put in carrots, celery and onions, which he had added this afternoon, so they wouldn't dissolve in the hot liquid. He topped everything off with a combination of his favorite spices: thyme, oregano, basil, tons of garlic, pepper and salt. Everyone lapped it up with crusts of flat bread, Manolo had been saving. Eventually Miguel finished and hurried up to the bridge, so that Bill could eat.

Bill came down and enjoyed the food immensely. He made a point to tell Manolo, "Good job, and thank you for making a hearty meal!" He took Manolo aside.

"Hey Manolo, how are you going to turn this into breakfast?"

Manolo smiled, "I'm going to serve it over toast and tortillas!"

"Thanks," said Bill.

Manolo shrugged his shoulders, "I can stir in some scrambled eggs, *Capitain* Bill!

"Bill smiled, "Yeah, that would be good. Good job, son!"

Everyone turned in to get some rest. Bill promised the day would likely be very lively. They needed to get some sleep. Bill pulled Jack aside, "Get some sleep Jack! Good chance we will see the girls tomorrow and we need you sharp and focused."

Jack nodded and went into the forecastle to sleep. Miguel was at the helm when Bill came up on deck. He was assigned to keep watch for the next six hours and to alert Bill if there was any activity on the water. Bill made it clear that if there was activity this far upstream, then there were likely to be lethal people involved. Miguel would drive for the next few hours, and then Bill would replace him.

Bill went below deck and opened his hatch to see Charlie

sitting on the edge of his bunk. He smiled, but his eyes were as big as saucers. Charlie smiled. "Welcome home sailor! Been a long cruise?"

Bill's face belied the terror he felt inside. He stood there in his own stateroom looking and shaking like an idiot.

Charlie smiled, "Shut the hatch, Bill." Bill turned and closed the watertight hatch. "Come here Bill." She patted the bunk and motioned for Bill to sit beside her. Bill, came over and sat down. He looked away, around and everywhere he could, but not at Charlie.

"My, my, my, Bill Treese. How long has it been?"

"Uh, too long. Too damn long." He looked at Charlie. She had shed her fatigues and was sitting in tight shorts and a workout top, which was very low cut and accentuated her ample figure. Bill suddenly noticed she had failed to wear a bra, which excited him, unexpectedly, to no end.

"Wow," he said, you really held up Charlie!" She smiled at him.

Bill stood up and said enthusiastically while clapping his hands, "Well! Time to hit the old sackaroo!"

Charlie laughed. "Bill, you still know how to charm the birds out of the trees! No, not really!"

Bill laughed, "Well, here's to old, but good times Charlie!"

They fell back into the bunk and kissed for a long time. Bill reached up and turned out the light over the bunk. The clock on his sea desk illuminated the cabin in an earthly green glow. It was hot, but there was a breeze from the fan mounted on the wall which blew quietly. Charlie whispered in the dark, "I never stopped loving you, Bill. I hate to admit that." She laid her head onto his chest.

Bill took a long, deep breath, feeling the loneliness and the pain of many years starting to fall away from him. His large hand caressed her shoulder. "Charlie, I've thought about you and loved you for the last four decades. Please stay safe tomorrow. I would die if I lost you again." The shadows grew long, and they became lovers once again in the dark.

****

Supreme General Juan Velasco pulled up in his jeep to the military outpost on the Atrato River. His men got off their troop carrier jeep, but only Velasco, his Lieutenant, and four of his men, boarded the boat. General de Luna, made great strides to welcome them aboard, but both parties knew they could be sacrificed by each other, as they might ultimately have different objectives.

As if by magic or reason, the two Generals embraced each other and vowed to work together to find the gold and to sell the girls to the highest bidder.

"Do we know the exact location of the mine," asked General de Luna.

"Mostly, but not exactly," said Supreme General Velasco. We are going to a tributary off the River Atrato but, because there are a couple of forks, we are going to have to use some of our dead reckoning skills to find the exact location of the mine." It was a lie. Juan Velasco didn't get to where he was by showing his entire hand all at once. He continued, "I have been given some good intel, but it may still be a bit of a crap shoot. Don't forget, finding the gold mine is the first problem. The second problem is we need to find a way inside, and then find the gold, if it is really there."

"What about the girls?" asked General de Luna.

"Ah, yes. Together, we may get around $500,000 to a million, for all of them. But the gold could be worth 100 million."

"True," said de Luna, "but we have the girls. They are money in our hands right now. The gold is only a possibility." He knew he had to watch his tone and what he said to a superior officer. But General de Luna had started to have doubts about Velasco sharing the gold with him and his men. He wanted to just get the hell off this river, go to Cartagena and sell their prisoners.

Supreme General Velasco shrugged his shoulders. "I want to meet the girls. Let's go below deck. Have your men bring them down to the galley. Don't scare them! We'll tell them a lie that will ease their minds."

General de Luna nodded. He gave the orders to his deck officer, while he and Juan Velasco went below deck to the small galley and sat down at the table. The quarters below deck were tight because of the shallow draft of the boat.

After a few minutes, they heard footsteps coming down the ladder. All four girls stood in front of the men. They stood uneasily as Juan Velasco looked them over. He smiled and said in English. "I don't want you girls to be afraid. We brought you here to hold you for ransom. We will be contacting your families and telling them how much they need to pay to get you back to them."

The girls, thinking they were going to be sold as slaves, visibly relaxed at his words, but only for a minute.

"Do you have any questions? And may I know each of

your names, please?"

Jazmine was the first to speak, "My name is Jazmine Paris, sir. We are afraid for our lives out here. We were thinking you were going to sell us into slavery. How will you contact our families? You don't really know us."

Juan Velasco, said, "We have told your teacher *Señor Roberto*, back in Colon, who is contacting them now. He will give them our demands, and they will raise the money and once it is deposited in our account, then we will make arrangements to have you transported back to the United States."

The girls looked at each other, Jackie, whose parents were from Puerto Rico, was unsure. "Sir, my name is Jackie Ricardo. My family does not have a lot of money, because they take care of my extended family back where they came from. What will we do, if they can't raise the ransom demands?"

Juan Velasco smiled. Her dark beauty intrigued him. "Where is your family from?" He could tell she was of Latin heritage. "They are from Puerto Rico, and we have many family members who rely on our help."

Juan glanced at General de Luna, who's face remained impassive and said nothing.

Juan looked at Jackie and smiled, "Don't worry about it, girl. We will work it out. We are making one demand for one amount. It is up to your families to pay as much as they can to get you back."

Gwendolyn was the next to speak. She was shy and very upset they had been put in this situation. "My name is Gwendolyn Jones. I don't have any questions, but I am afraid you will hurt us and maybe," she hesitated, "you might take advantage of us," she said in a small voice.

Supreme General Velasco waved his hand dismissively, as if that was the last thing on their minds, and said, "You have nothing to worry about girl! You are worth money to us unharmed and unmolested. We want money for you, not sex! The crew have been given strict orders not to molest you in any way. If we wanted that, we would not have gone to the trouble to drag you through this damn jungle. Isn't that right, General?"

General de Luna nodded his head, but again said nothing.

Juan Velasco looked at the last girl. She was a dark blonde, and kept tossing her long hair back from her face. She looked to have a very brash attitude. Juan liked feisty girls. "And you?" he asked. "My name is Cazzy Carmichael. I want to know, was *Señor Roberto* in on this? Was he a part of it?"

Both of the men laughed. "Of course, he was!" said Juan Velasco. "I went to school with him. He was my best friend! He dated my cousin! He needed money because of his gambling problems. He hand-picked each one of you! His debts will all be paid, and he is going to be a very rich man and live down here with us once this is all over!"

At that news, all four of the girls began to cry. They felt betrayed, angry and hurt. They and their parents had been duped by him after all!

General de Luna spoke up for the first time, "We are going to take you downriver and once we have the money demanded, we will drop you off near the airport. We won't accompany you for obvious reasons. We would advise you not to talk to anyone. There will be a man there, who we have hired to give you your tickets. The airport is at Cartagena, where you will board a direct flight back home. The less you say to anyone, the safer you will be.

Any questions?"

The girl's tears had turned to sobs, but they now had hope they would be released to their families, even though they still had doubts. They felt safer if they stayed together.

General de Luna turned to his deck officer, who had been standing behind the girls. In Spanish, he said, "Go ahead and take them back to the deck and put them under the canvas, once they have used the bathroom." See if they want any snacks before bed."

Once the girls had returned to the deck, the two generals began to talk quietly together.

Juan Velasco said, "We will be at the tributary in the morning. I have decided to not spend more than a day at the mine. I want to sell these girls quickly. Now that I have seen them, I believe we can sell them for more than I thought. So, as you say, the bird in the hand is worth two in the bush, *eh amigo!*"

Xavier de Luna smiled. "Good," he said, "I believe we are on the same page now. Let's eat and get to the tributary!"

General de Luna gave the order to his deck officer, and they shoved off down the river, into the early dusk and the setting sun.

****

It was 0600. The PT boat had reached the tributary. The crew had risen early and eaten quickly. They had reported to Bill formally, and he had each one of them put on a helmet and life jacket. When he came to Zenadia, she just giggled at him. She was still wearing the jungle camouflage skirt and tight black top. "I'm good," she smiled at Bill. He just shook his head, knowing not to argue with her.

Jack was on the port machine gun, John was on the starboard machine gun and Manolo was at the Oerlikon Cannon in the stern. Miguel was in the engine compartment, making sure all three engines would run properly. Charlie and Zenadia were on the bridge with Bill. They waited, hoping they would see something. There were a few more vessels on the river this early morning, but not many. The boat was at idle. If they didn't see anything, Bill would head up the tributary and begin searching for any boat that looked like a military boat. Right now, he was scanning up and back down the river. The PT boat was pointed upriver, which made it easier to see the oncoming traffic. *This was such a crapshoot,* he thought. *We need a ton of luck right now!*

CHAPTER EIGHT

THE LOST GOLD MINE OF THE DARIÉN GAP

JAZMINE PARIS REALLY HAD TO USE THE bathroom. It was early in the morning. The boat had been traveling all night. She heard the heavy footsteps of the sentry walking back and forth on the deck near her. She carefully poked her head out and saw him. He was walking away from her. She whispered, *"¡Señor, señor!"*

He turned around and immediately came over to her. He kneeled down to her. In Spanish she begged him to please take her below to the bathroom. She used her nicest, most pleading voice with him. He replied in Spanish that he would. He whistled to another soldier to come and watch the girls while he took her below. He told Jazmine to wait for a minute. He descended down the ladder to the lower deck. General de Luna was drinking coffee and looking at a map in the galley. Supreme General Velasco was still in his sea cabin, just waking up.

The sentry, came over and asked the General for permission

to bring her down to use the head. Without looking up or saying anything, de Luna, waved his hand signaling that it was OK. The girls had been polite and cooperative. The men had nothing to fear from them.

The sentry returned to the girls and reached down to help Jazmine up. She walked in front of him, down the ladder and past General de Luna to use the bathroom. "Don't take too long," the soldier said to her in Spanish.

****

Bill was still scanning with his powerful binoculars up the river, from where he thought they might be coming. He had actually let his boat drift a little further upstream, so that the tributary was slightly behind him, by about a hundred yards. Suddenly he saw it. 1000 yards upstream, a combat boat that had maybe 4-5 feet of draft, outfitted with what looked like single .50 caliber machine guns and possibly heavier weapons, was moving toward them, but on the opposite side of the river. The river was about a quarter-mile wide here. He wasn't sure, but it was the only one he had seen that resembled something the girls might be on. It was going to pass them, about 40 yards to their left side.

Suddenly, Zenadia turned to Bill and said matter-of-factly, "There's your boat!"

Right then the boat began to pass them and make a turn to the tributary. At that moment, Jazmine appeared on deck, walking in front of the sentry, who was taking her back to the stern to join her friends. Jack, in the port gun turret, saw her. At that instant, for no reason at all, Jazmine turned her head to the right. She suddenly saw the PT boat and locked eyes with her dad. Time froze for an instant. She screamed, "Daddeeeeee!" Beside himself, Jack screamed, "Jazmine!"

Bill, grabbing the wheel with one hand, instantly lit up all three engines and mashed the throttle forward with the other hand. The PT boat accelerated with a huge roar, as if shot out of a slingshot, and Bill spun the wheel madly to the left, propelling the heavy PT boat to the port and almost giving Jack a bath as the rails on the left side of the boat dipped below the water. Manolo, Charlie and Zenadia hung on, while, below deck, Miguel was flung on the inside of the boat, against the wall. He was dazed but conscious. He shook his head to clear it and hurried up the stern ladder to see what was going on. "Game on!" cried Bill. "Let's see what you've got now you bastards!"

The Panamanian war boat had suddenly throttled up and was picking up speed. It could go about the same speed as the PT boat, but was more maneuverable and had a smaller draft, meaning it could travel up shallower waters without getting stuck. General de Luna rushed up on deck, followed by Supreme General Velasco, still buttoning his pants and tucking in his shirt.

"What the hell is happening?" yelled de Luna to his deck officer, who turned around and pointed at the American PT boat which was chasing them up the tributary.

The sentry had grabbed Jazmine and dragged her up to the cockpit, while the other sentry kept a gun aimed at the other girls, who were still under the canvas tarp, laying on the deck in the stern. The one held Jazmine tightly by her arms. Juan Velasco asked her angrily, who the hell are they?"

Jazmine smiled. She had to yell above the roar of the engines, "That's a World War II PT boat! That's my dad on that boat and he is really pissed off right now! Good time for you to surrender! That boat can blow you clean out of the water in about two seconds!" She smiled, "Get ready for it!"

Just then, they heard a volley of machine gun fire from the PT boat. The tracers showed the bullets, even in this early dawn hour, passing harmlessly over their heads as a warning. General de Luna barked orders at his helmsman and the rest of the crew.

Juan Velasco said to Jazmine, "They won't blow us up, because you girls are onboard!" Suddenly a second burst of machine gun fire flew over their heads.

General de Luna yelled at his gunners to return fire. They had two single mount .50 caliber machine guns on either side of the boat. They also had a rocket launcher, but it had malfunctioned on the last mission, and they did not trust it. Suddenly the PT boat had to juke back and forth, as the Panamanian boat returned fire.

Bill Treese had installed Kevlar and steel around the bridge, gun turrets and the Oerlikon Cannon, so they were relatively safe, as long as they did not expose themselves. "Stop firing!" yelled Bill. "We can't take a chance of hitting the girls!" Charlie ran into the chart house and down the ladder to Bill's sea cabin. She opened up her back pack and pulled out her military sharpshooter rifle. She ran back up to the cockpit. She yelled at Bill that she wanted to take a crack at the shooters. He nodded. Standing in the cockpit, next to Bill, she set up the rifle quickly and took aim at the gunner on the port side of the boat. Bill was still zig zagging to avoid their fire.

"You have to hold her steady for 5 seconds!" she yelled.

Bill straightened the boat out, while Charlie took careful aim. *Stick you head up, sunshine,* she thought. The soldier came into her view just as he was about to fire off another volley at the PT boat. She depressed the trigger and a single round shot him in the head. He fell back dying instantly. No more than three seconds passed, and she shot the soldier on the starboard side, who died, as well.

General de Luna, shocked at seeing his men being picked off so easily, screamed orders at two of his men. One grabbed a fully automatic AK-47 rifle and ran back toward the stern firing his weapon at the pursuing PT boat. Another soldier ran behind him and whipped off the tarp that had been covering the three girls. The girls screamed as he sat them up in the stern of the boat and squatted behind them, holding his own rifle.

Bill saw this and yelled at Charlie, "Cease fire! They are using the girls as human shields! Bastards!" They could see the three young girls sitting in the stern of the boat, who were screaming with fear from the chase and the shooting all around them.

"What are we going to do?" Jack yelled over to Bill, while keeping an eye on his daughter, who was still being held in the cockpit.

"We're going to follow them. The mine is up ahead somewhere, and I think they will stop there, in spite of our presence. They know we won't approach them, because they might hurt the girls. I only hope the water is deep enough to support us, because their draft is less, and they can go farther upriver than we can."

"How will we know?" asked Jack.

"The PT boat has sonar to scan upriver, so that it should warn us in plenty of time, if there is a sandbar or shallow water ahead of us. The worst thing that can happen is if we rip out the bottom of our hull! We would be goners!"

Both boats continued to sail upriver without shots being fired. Bill had kept a tight distance from the Panamanian boat and did not waver. The dense jungle passed them by on both sides. They came to a fork in the river and Bill knew the left branch was the correct route from his discussions with Maltilda. Sure enough, the enemy vessel steered left, and Bill followed suit.

They had traveled about a mile when Bill's underwater sonar began pinging, indicating they were about to enter water which was too shallow to support the PT boat. He began to slow down, and the two generals on the Panamanian boat noted this with surprise and happiness. Jack, alarmed, said to Bill, "What are you doing? They are getting away!"

"It's too shallow, Jack! We can't go any farther upriver or we will play out and be sitting ducks!" Bill came to a full stop and the men on the escaping boat let out a loud cheer. The four kidnapped girls, thinking they had a chance to be rescued, all let out a groan of despair. The appearance of the PT boat had given them hope, but that was gone now. The soldier that was holding them had retreated to the Bridge to get further instructions.

Gwendolyn said to Cazzy, "Why did they stop?"

Cazzy said, "The river is too shallow. They can't follow us!"

"Damnit!" said Jackie. "Why are they keeping Jazmine on the Bridge?"

Cazzy said, "Because that is the PT boat her dad's friend owns. The one that we were supposed to get a ride on, when our trip was over. How the hell they found us in this God-forsaken jungle is a mystery to me. But even if they had to pull out, you can bet it is only temporary, because they will be like a dog on a bone. They won't rest or stop, until they get us away from these bad people."

Gwendolyn asked, "Did you believe them when they said we would be freed once our parents paid a ransom?"

Cazzy snorted, "Hell no girl! Those mo fo's are going to sell us to the highest bidders. Maybe a Sheikh, or a playboy down here in South America. Didn't you ever watch the movie, *Taken?* Shit, that stuff is real. Kidding me? 18-year-old American girls?! Shoot, we are worth a million bucks to them! Maybe more! Plus, them fuckers will all want to take a turn with us before they sell us. Why not? What do they have to lose?"

Suddenly, realizing she had been a little too blunt, as Gwendolyn began to cry, seeing the hopelessness of the situation, Cazzy put her arm around Gwen. "Stop girl! The good guys have spotted us. Do you think they are going to give up without a fight? Not gonna' happen! OK?" Gwen nodded, but put her face into her arms, which were crossed over her bent knees. She continued to weep, wishing she could see her mom, her dad, her little brother, Jason and their two golden retriever dogs, Moose and Gabriel. *Life had gone to hell in a handbasket*, she thought.

General de Luna and Supreme General Velasco, welcomed the PT boat's inability to chase them as a reason to celebrate. "She can't continue upriver, Xavier!" Velasco cried triumphantly. "We are free to pursue our quest to go to the gold mine and then take these girls to our friends to sell them!"

General de Luna was not so confident. "Sir, we must take

precautions. Now may not be the time to search for the Lost Gold Mine! True, she cannot follow, as the water is not deep enough, but they could launch a land expedition, or sail back downstream to engage us on the Atrato, before we have completed our quest. Sir, this tributary has a loop that will send us around all hostilities, and then land us back on a crossing river, shallow still, that will send us way downriver back on the Atrato River. That will place us beyond their evil clutches!"

"So, you say, so, you say," said Supreme General Juan Velasco, stroking his chin thoughtfully. He looked his general in the eye. "That is an excellent plan. They are effectively neutralized at this point, so I say, let us proceed to the mines, find a way in, take out the gold and then move forward as you have instructed!"

General de Luna nodded, then he sighed. He thought, *his commander was still not grasping the gravity of the situation. They could still be caught by the men on the PT boat, as they had the best motivation in the world-the return of their loved ones!*

Bill Treese was not going to be outwitted by these Third-World dictators. He intended to return to the branch they had passed one mile back down the river. The chart indicated it was deeper and actually looped back around to the river they had had to bypass. The two rivers ran parallel to each other and were separated by several miles of dense jungle, according to the map. But, since the first one was too shallow to enter, logic would dictate that the one at the top half of the map would be even more shallow. However, there could be a sandbar blocking the first one. You never knew until you tried! In anger and frustration, Bill, once again spun the wheel to the left and slammed the three throttle levers, representing the three engines, forward. The three Packard engines roared to life and the PT boat spun on its heels and turned left, speeding back down the tributary as if in surrender!

Once again, the Generals and the crew on the Panamanian boat let loose a roar, as they knew the Americans had been defeated! General Velasco, shoved Jazmine back off the Bridge and yelled for the sentry to take her back to the rest of the girls. "Cover them up," he screamed at the guards, "Cover them up and let's proceed to the mines of gold! *Adelante amigos!*" With a shout the crew engaged with their Generals and the boat roared upstream toward the lost gold mine!

****

The PT boat had hit the branch on the tributary, made a hard turn left and drove up the new river with a vengeance. The crew had seen the girls, been thwarted by their pursuit, and were now bearing down on their position. They had decided they would get the girls out at all costs. There would be no parliamentary discussions, no reasoning, no bullshit agreements, no taking of prisoners. Those people who held the girls would simply die. End of story.

As they roared up the river, now being driven by Miguel, Jack, John and Bill, poured over the jungle map in the small galley below deck. Bill spoke up, "We can get up to the loop, circle around and get back to the mine in about a day, or maybe a day and a half. They can continue upstream, bypass the mine and get past us to the Atrato River, and we will never find them. Or, they can reverse their course, forget about the mine and get to the Atrato River, escape downstream, sell the girls and be done with it."

Jack spoke up, "Why can't I jump ship and go across the jungle to the Lost Mine. They would never expect a land attack, while you guys go up and around. There is a lot to be said about a land attack, coupled with a sea attack!"

Bill shook his head, "Jack, you wouldn't make it one mile in this fuckin' jungle. There are too many bad guys waiting for you to simply fuck up, and then you belong to them. Then, guess what? There are deadly snakes, spiders, crocodiles, caimans, snakes, did I mention snakes? There is nothing out here that wouldn't like a nice tasty white man snack! "Yeah," answered Jack, "But maybe saving my daughter compels me to continue to do things I would never, ever do in this lifetime. Right?!"

Bill shook his head. Jack spoke up again, "When you are at a spot perpendicular to the mine, please come to a stop and I will set out to save my little girl."

Bill nodded. John didn't say anything. He was frightened out of his mind. This was worse than him being lost in the mine and almost drowning, worse that everything they had experienced before.

Bill spoke up, "I'll go with you and we will can these bastards!"

"No, you won't," said a voice from the ladder leading down to the galley. "I'll go with Jack." It was Zenadia.

The men looked at each other. Jack spoke up, "Zenadia, we appreciate your help so far in this and," he looked at Bill and John, "it has been immense. We would never have made it this far without you, and never made it with what we know without you. But this is not your fight. You have a right to a better life away from here. I don't want to take a chance of you being killed."

Zenadia smiled. "Jack, Jack, Jack!" she said. "Jack! This isn't about you! It isn't about me!" All the men in the galley were staring at her. "Jack, you wouldn't last a day in this jungle! Who is going to take you in? John? Bill? Ha Ha! You are both a couple of chubby wussies compared to me!" Both Bill and John smiled with a mixture of humiliation and the realization that she was right. They didn't say anything.

Zenadia continued, "Jack, I'm going in with you to get the girls out. Don't worry, I'll protect you and them."

"Ok," said Jack, looking at the skirt and the tight black tank top, Zenadia was wearing, "Don't you think you should dress in something a little more, uh, battle-worthy?"

"No Jack, I wear what I wear. You are all visitors. I am one with the jungle, its creatures and all its inhabitants. You are the outsiders. I am the insider that will get you and your family back. But, once we are out there, make no mistake, I am in command. You will do exactly as I say, because there are lives in the balance. Not mine! I will always survive. Only yours, your daughter's, and the other girls. Do you understand and agree?"

Jack nodded. He didn't say anything.

"Good," said Zenadia. "Get your weapons and let's move out!"

Bill had moved his PT boat up the river to a spot, which he deemed to be approximately parallel to the mine's location, several miles away. Jack was on deck in jungle fatigues, sturdy boots and a camouflaged helmet. His face was covered in camouflage paint. He had a fully automatic AK-47 rifle, which had two extended magazines taped end to end, each holding a total of 60 rounds. It could be set to fire one shot, a burst of three shots, or fully automatic. He had a Baretta 9mm handgun, which held 16 rounds. He also had a survival knife and a machete on his belt. He was carrying a backpack which held two drum magazines for the AK-47, with 100 rounds each. He had two canteens of water, which Bill had given him, and six hand grenades to wear on his belt. He was wearing a Kevlar bullet-proof vest under his fatigues, which protected his torso. He also had a bandanna around his face to protect him from the thousands of mosquitos flying around.

Because of his combat gear, he knew he would be extremely hot in the jungle, but comfort had to take a back seat to safety. There was one other factor: Jack was a martial artist trained in the Bruce Lee technique of Jeet Kune Do. He had skills. He had packed his telescoping metal nunchakus, metal throwing stars with sharp edges and carved darts, that he could hurl at the enemy at will. These weapons were always close at hand, stored on his body.

In contrast, Zenadia, on the deck, was only wearing her same jungle print skirt and tight black top. She had on light running shoes and no socks.

Charlie was on the port machinegun, John on the starboard gun, while Manolo was manning the Oerlikon Cannon. Miguel and Kimmi were on the bridge, with binoculars, looking for anything that could help or hurt them. They were on either side of Bill, who was driving the boat.

"We're here, Jack," Bill" said.

Jack and Zenadia came forward to Bill on the Bridge. It was quite a contrast. Jack looked like he was heading into a jungle mission in Viet Nam, and Zenadia looked like she was headed for a picnic. Zenadia looked at Jack's camouflaged face. She smiled, "Nice makeup Jack." Jack looked at her sideways, but didn't say anything. "Don't worry, Jack, I can get those girls back with one spell tied behind my back!" Jack smiled at that, but kept his game face on.

Bill giggled for a second, not to insult Jack, who was here to save his daughter, but because Zenadia seemed so unaffected, so relaxed, almost like she was going to bend any situation to her will and come out on top.

Jack, said, "What are you laughing at?"

"Nothing Jack. Maybe just that Zenadia is so damn nonchalant? I don't know. I hope you both have success. In the meantime, we will be driving up the tributary and making the loop that circles back down the river to try to intercept the bad guys at the Lost Mine. Charlie wants to go with you, but I want her here. If the girls stay onboard the boat, I need a sharpshooter with me. We may be forced to pick off those bastards on the deck one by one, and I need Charlie to do that for me." Charlie looked over at them and smiled. She looked at her daughter Zenadia and mouthed, "I love you!" to her. Zenadia smiled back at her and mouthed, "Don't worry!" They had their own means of communicating with each other. Charlie nodded and returned to looking up and down the river for any hostilities.

Jack nodded at Bill. The PT boat moved over to the shore. Jack and Zenadia, jumped over the rails and landed on the sand. Without hesitation, they dashed off into the jungle!

They made up over a mile in about an hour, but the further they traveled, the denser the jungle became. The vines and the undergrowth began to dwarf the trees, making it nearly impossible to pass. They moved slowly up the thin specter of the trail toward the lost gold mine.

****

General de Luna and Supreme General Velasco were on the bridge of their vessel, moving slowly upriver. They were looking at an old map of the region and a small antique book, with a cracked leather cover. It was a diary of one of the original explorers of the mine from the 1800's. He had described the mine and its entrance. However, he wrote that the mine was played out and did not contain any gold. The account was valuable, in that it described important landmarks that stood out from the rest of the terrain, which is what they needed.

General Velasco spoke up first, "Xavier, what did you see in the drawings?"

"A large peak, sir, surrounded by two more smaller peaks. That is the treasure mine!"

"OK, how will we access it then? They say the entrance is under water?"

"No Supreme General, there is another opening on the other side. It used to be covered by rocks, but the latest data shows it has been unearthed by recent violent rain and storms. There was also a small earthquake recently. It is good fortune that we may be able to access it, since decades of others have been denied!"

"We will go there and find the treasure, Xavier!" shouted General Velasco.

CHAPTER NINE

THE LOST WARRIOR TRIBE

THEY WERE THE MEN AND WOMEN OF THE small tribes. Theirs was a secret society, hidden away from the rest of the world. Most of them were less than five feet tall, but they were strong and mighty. Fierce warriors of another time, their sacred duty was to guard the treasure. Their tribe had been here for over 400 years and they survived by hunting and gathering, as well as farming. Their one mandate was to protect the treasure, once taken out of the Darién Gap by Spanish Conquistadors, then transferred to Spain. Their history was rich with legends of killing scores of fortune hunters through the centuries. Every man, woman and child had been sworn from birth to protect hundreds of gold bricks. Why? No one knew. The gold was useless to them, as they needed food and medicine, not gold. But they had simply followed the path of their ancestors and deemed the gold as their deity, to protect against all transgressors. And, being men and women of faith, their commitment never wavered.

The tribe was led by Jojo, who was 89 years old. His mate was Sulu, also 89. They were there when the gold seekers came in 1946. They heard the decree by the elders and when the men came, they witnessed their destruction. The shaman told them the brick stolen by the white men would be returned soon. How this would happen was not known, but they did know that their tribe would not be whole again until the final brick was deposited. Until then, they would be ready to kill all enemies, to keep their faith.

Jojo and Sulu sat in the chamber looking at the stacks of gold bars. They had been elected by the tribe to lead, because of Jojo's ferociousness and Sulu's maternal love and instincts for the tribe. Their lives had been devoted to simply guarding the gold, hunting, growing the crops and raising the next generation to protect the sacred gold. Now, they were facing their greatest challenge in years and had many difficult choices to make. Were they to move forward and embrace a new world that restoration of the missing gold might bring, or simply repeat the old practice of killing any intruders, as had their parents and their parents before them had done?

Jojo, thought back. He glanced over at his wife, his mate, his best friend Sulu. Just as pretty now as she had been when they were children.

They loved each other fiercely. Jojo and Sulu had been together since they were 14 years old. Defying their parents, they refused arranged marriages to others and stood their ground, drawing their lines in the sand. It was not pretty.

Both were 14 and had been arranged to marry others they did not love, because of tradition and family obligations. Jojo was supposed to marry a girl, named Cinta, who was vicious, mean and four years his senior. She was much bigger than him and Sulu. Sulu was supposed to marry a fierce warrior, named Lorame, a tribe favorite who was 20. He towered over both her and Jojo.

By refusing the contracted marriages, Jojo and Sulu placed their lives in forfeit. Jojo challenged Lorame to a fight to the death for the hand of Sulu. The entire tribe was in attendance when he made the announcement. The three Elders and Jojo's own father said if he lost, he would be put to death, even if he didn't die in the fight. Jojo responded that when he won the fight, he would kill all three of the Elders and kill his own father too, which enraged everyone. Jojo had no remorse. He had no feelings, no loyalty, no mercy. He only had one thing that was stronger than anything else; he loved Sulu and that was his power, his obsession. He would kill anyone who got in his way!

The Elders said that once Jojo was defeated, they would let Cinta take her revenge against Sulu, and beat the girl within a slip of her life. Sulu, in total defiance of the tribal Elders said that once the fight began between her true love, Jojo, and Lorame, who she hated, she would attack Cinta and kill her just to make a point.

The situation was tense and everyone knew that many lives were at stake!

The next day, the tribe assembled in the clearing behind the chamber of gold. Two hundred natives yelled, chanted and beat their drums.

Jojo, flanked by his six most loyal and trusted friends, came out and stood on the edge of the clearing. Suddenly, Lorame, six years older, 60 pounds heavier, and 12 inches taller, burst into the clearing! Running around the perimeter of the clearing, he screamed like an animal, then ran straight at Jojo! He grabbed Jojo, hit him over and over, then flung him like a rag doll over his head into the trees! Jojo collapsed, while his friends ran up to him and picked him up. His best friend Alia, pulled him up and shook him awake. "Fight!" he screamed in their native language. "You have to kill him or be killed!" Jojo snapped awake, and when Lorame charged him again to finish the job, Jojo grabbed Lorame's arms, rolled onto his back, and kicked him in the testicles, as he tossed him over his head and onto his back!

Lorame screamed and lay in the sand clutching his manhood. Driven by fury, lust and the smell of blood, Jojo ran over and began to beat Lorame with a viciousness never seen by these tribesmen. He suddenly dashed over, grabbed an ax from one of the surprised guardsmen and ran over to chop Lorame in half! As he raised the ax high, the elders, as one, screamed at him to stop. Jojo held up as Lorame looked up, his head at a perfect angle.

Jojo turned to the three Elders and his father, who stood by them. All of 14 years old, he bravely stood tall before the entire tribe. One of the Elders said, "Jojo! Enough! You are free to marry who you want! Please do not kill this boy, who we love, and wish to spare." The other Elder and Jojo's father both nodded in agreement, but the Center Elder who was the highest in rank, except for the Chief, said, "No! He has defied the Tribe and must die! Even though he has won, he must die!"

In a moment, which would be spoken of for the next six decades, Jojo smiled, turned toward him and hurled the ax directly at the Elder, striking him in the chest and killing him!

With a gasp, no one dared move. Jojo walked over to Sulu

and took her hand. He led her into the center of the circle. He yelled at the top of his lungs, "If any man, or," he stared directly at Cinta, "any woman wants to challenge the love between Sulu and I, please come forward, so I can kill you as well! I spit on this Elder! If anyone here interferes with our love, then I curse you and," citing a feared curse from the region, he said ***"May the Great Worm of Death gnaw at your exposed entrails, and may all your bones now rot in death joint by joint!"***

Several of the women screamed and fainted. The men drew covers over their faces to protect themselves. No one moved to pick up the Elder who Jojo had killed. Lorame pushed himself up and put his hands up to Jojo. "I don't want her!" he said over and over. "She belongs to you!" Cinta, for her part, screamed and, covering her head, ran into the jungle and did not reappear for weeks.

Only the arrival of the Chief and his Medicine Man, calmed the situation. Jojo and Sulu, two fourteen-year-old children, who had been forced to grow up too soon, stood defiantly in the middle of the clearing. No one spoke. Finally, the Chief, in his infinite wisdom, declared, "Jojo has won the right to marry Sulu. As he has stated, if anyone defies this marriage, then they shall be subject to the great curse he has laid before us!"

The Medicine Man whispered something to the Chief.

The Chief continued, "I will honor this matrimony, when the time is right. Also, since I have not been blessed with children, I decree that Jojo and his wife will rule this tribe, once my eyes have closed and I am transported to the great beyond."

The tribe, stunned, began to cheer for Jojo and his soon-to-be bride, Sulu, in celebration of the breaking of an old tradition. They knew there would no longer be any more arranged marriages, because Jojo would never allow it.

At the age of 16, Jojo and Sulu were married and at the age of 20, Jojo became the Chief. He ruled for decades, earning the love of his tribe, as did his wife Sulu, who was the kind mother to them all. To the tribe, they were loved, but to outsiders, they would deal death to keep their tribe whole.

The light from the torches illuminated the gold chamber and the smoke stung their nostrils. The Shaman joined them in the gold chamber. He bowed low, before the Chief and his wife. "Give me your bidding my masters," he said.

Chief Jojo was succinct. "What do you know and what do you see? We are relying on your instincts for our lives. We can fend off anyone, but is that what we should do? We may have an opportunity, as you have said to get our brick back, which would make us whole again."

"May I speak freely, my master?"

"Yes!" Jojo gestured emphatically, suddenly growing impatient.

"Then I will tell you all that I see. The one called Maltilda, who carried out our brick, has given it to another; a white man who cares nothing about the gold. The white man and others he is with, seek the return of their children, who have been taken by evil people of the civilization. Both groups attack each other in their great boats with their great guns of war.

"A friend of the man with the brick travels here in the jungle. He is also a white man."

"Wait," said Jojo, "you said a white man is coming here.

Through the jungle? By himself? He will be eaten alive! Is he a fool?"

"No, Great One. He is a father. A father of one of the kidnapped girls. He travels here to find her and take her away from the bad people."

Jojo snorted, "He is still a fool to come through the jungle. He will die in vain for his daughter and the big cats will thank him!"

"He does not travel alone, my Master."

"Who then?"

"The young witch who we have spoken of in many tales of the Amazon."

"No, not Z! She is dead, killed at the hands of the Chibchas!"

"No. She was not killed. They say she was exorcised and the devil was driven out of her. Only to lay waste to the jungle surrounding the Chibchas!"

"No, I don't believe it!" said Jojo.

The Shaman shrugged.

"Who told you this?" demanded Jojo.

"My cousin, who is related to the Chibchas. His uncle was there and said the demons came out of her and everyone saw it. She stayed for many months and then left on the very boat that is down here to find the girls!"

Jojo didn't say anything for a long time. Finally, he said, "Does the girl still have powers?"

The Shaman shrugged again without speaking.

"Thank you, said Jojo, "I will ponder this and decide how we shall act."

The Shaman bowed and exited. Jojo looked at his wife Sulu, who looked back at him with a smile meant to be their hopeful salvation. Jojo nodded and looked over at the gold stack with its one missing brick.

****

Jack and Zenadia made their way carefully through the thick jungle. Zenadia was leading the way, sliding effortlessly through the heavy growth, while Jack had to hack his way through the vines and branches with his machete. Jack felt eyes on him, almost the moment they got off the boat. The sounds of the jungle were all around them. There was the screech of monkeys, birds and the occasional growl of predators, probably jaguars. After they had trekked a second mile, which took the better part of two and a half hours, Jack called to Zenadia to stop for a minute to rest. Zenadia smiled and stopped in a small clearing. Jack labored up to her and sat down on the large root of a giant Kapok tree. He pulled out one of his canteens and drank the cool water. All around him, it was hot, steamy and humid, made all the worse by Jack's jungle fatigues. He offered his canteen of water to Zenadia, who shook her head. Jack was amazed; she did not sweat or even look hot.

"Aren't you hot?" he asked. She shook her head. "This is my home."

Jack shook his head. After a minute, he said, "I guess we better move out."

Zenadia nodded and they resumed their quest for the Lost Gold Mine.

****

General de Luna, Supreme General Velasco, and their crew moved upriver slowly. They were marking all of the landmarks on the old maps they had, comparing them with the landscape before them. They were almost upon what appeared to be the Lost Gold Mine. There was a bend in the river, and they emerged in a deep channel, with giant mountain peaks on either side of them. According to the maps they had, the only mountain on their right held a promise to yield gold. The one on the left was full of "Fool's Gold," or pyrite. Suddenly, they saw it. "Stop! Stop!" called General de Luna to his helmsman. Over their heads, was the mountain, with the waterfall and, they could see the lagoon, several meters away. The helmsman stopped the boat and General de Luna, Supreme General Velasco, and four of their men got out of the boat and jumped onto the shore. Six others soldiers also jumped off and spread out into the jungle behind them to stop anyone who tried to attack from that direction. From where they were, they could see their boat, but were hidden from the river. The remaining two soldiers would stay on the boat and watch the girls. In spite of the river being deeper upstream than downstream, they still felt they were safe from the PT boat because it was many kilometers behind them and had too deep of a draft to get this far upstream.

Suddenly, Supreme General Velasco yelled back at the guards to bring the girl Jazmine up. She would go with them and if anyone showed up to defend her, they would be met with death! Two of the soldiers went back and yanked Jazmine up by the arm and dragged her off the boat, while her friends screamed in protest. But, in spite of the pain, the fear and the unknown,

Jazmine refused to scream. Instead, she channeled her energy in a way to fight back against these bastards! She knew her dad was somewhere nearby and would sacrifice his life to protect her! She smiled in anticipation. There was going to be a savage fight and she would be sure to get her licks in as best as she could! Whatever she did, she had to make sure the channel to help them was open to her dad and the people on the PT boat.

As a group, they walked up to the edge of the lagoon. "Here is where the last expedition in 1946 entered the water," said de Luna. "But we now have a better way around the side. It is about 1,000 meters. Come, *Adelante!*"

The two generals, the four soldiers and Jazmine walked around the side of the mountain, picking their way through the jungle, looking for an opening that would lead them inside. Fortunately, there were no booby traps, snares or dead falls to encounter. They made their way to the base of the mountain, then went back and forth, looking for the entrance to the Lost Mine. After an hour, they finally saw a break in the rocks, which looked more like a landslide, than a natural opening.

Calling his men up front, General de Luna, spoke to them, saying he, Supreme General Velasco, Jazmine, plus the four soldiers would go inside. They had to turn sideways to enter the chamber and walked forward carefully. It was pitch black inside, and 30 degrees cooler than the jungle. The men all turned on their flashlights, while shivering in the sudden cold air. Two of the soldiers were in front, behind them were General de Luna, Supreme General Velasco and Jazmine. The final two soldiers were trailing behind, guarding their rear. The path was less than three meters wide and had walls of stone on either side.

Water trickled down the walls, forming small pools and puddles on the floor. They were forced to slosh through some standing water, about four inches deep. It felt as if they were moving downhill, and the longer they proceeded, the cooler it got. For a while, they appeared to move in a wide circular pattern, then straight for what felt like the length of a football field. Then they circled again, but now they were going in the opposite direction. It still felt like they were moving slightly downhill, and it continued getting colder.

Supreme General Velasco stopped and put up his hand. Everyone stopped. "Where is this tunnel leading us?" he asked General de Luna. He flashed his light over his head to the ceiling, which was approximately 15 meters high at this point.

General de Luna held up the tattered remains of his map, which was more helpful getting them to the mountain, but had very few clues how to get to the treasure once they were inside. He looked up at Supreme General Velasco and shrugged. "We must keep going forward until we find something or someone," he said. They both turned and indicated to the two soldiers leading them that they should continue moving forward.

Suddenly, they turned a corner and walked into an antechamber 15 meters wide by 15 meters long. In stark contrast, it was lit by torches which burned intensely. They shut off their flashlights, knowing they were finally about to come face to face with someone or something. They saw an opening at the end of the room and walked toward it. Carefully, the two soldiers in front looked through the opening and then, motioning towards the rest of the group, moved forward. They entered a larger chamber, which was well lit by torches and also natural light from above. It was then they saw it.

Stacks and stacks of gold bricks, dusty, but still shiny, obviously 24 karat gold, towered over six feet high, ten feet deep and twenty feet wide. The Generals and their soldiers gasped at the sheer magnitude of the value of the wealth before them. Jazmine, for her part, couldn't care less. She only wanted to get out of this damn chamber and find her father, who she knew would be searching for her. She also wanted to get her friends out of there as well and onto the safety of the PT boat.

The men moved forward. General de Luna said, "There is no one to fear now! Let us make our move and take this gold back to our *hombres* on the shore! We can send more to our *comandantes* who will be expecting more of the treasure!" They all moved forward, except Jazmine held back beyond the perimeter. The soldiers and the two Generals began to grab the gold bars and throw them into their backpacks over and over, not realizing that their packs may wind up being more than they could carry.

Watching them in the shadows were Jojo's tribesmen, carrying spears, darts, blow guns, and bows and arrows. They had moved in silently, but were told to just watch for now and not interfere. Tiny by modern standards, they were all less than five feet tall, but armed to the teeth. They were fierce and ready to tend to business, but all in good time. They watched as the men took as much of the gold as they could carry out.

Zenadia and Jack continued their trek through the jungle. They had to slow their approach some, because of the heat and density of the foliage as they neared the mountain. Zenadia stopped in a small clearing and pointed up and ahead of them. Jack looked up and saw the thin spire of a mountain towering over the trees. The sides were covered with some kind of green moss, as the sides were too steep to support any trees. It rose over one thousand feet and looked to be about 5 miles away.

Jack looked around. The jungle leaned in on them menacingly. The heat and humidity were almost unbearable. Just breathing and trying to swallow hurt Jack's throat. It looked all but impossible to get through the thick overgrowth. "How are we going to get through this jungle?" he asked Zenadia.

She shrugged, "Difficult but not impossible. There is a way. I don't know it exactly. I am trying to focus on a clearer path. I can make it through alright, but it is going to be more difficult for you, and that's why I am here. I want to get you back to your daughter." She paused, "By the way, once we get to the gold mine, there may be some not so nice people waiting for us."

Sure, I know that. You mean the soldiers who are holding our girl's prisoners, right?"

"Uh, no actually. There may be some pretty fierce natives who live there and guard the gold."

"What?" asked Jack, "How do you know that?"

Jungles all over the world whisper their secrets," she smiled, "and the jungle is my home. Maybe we will get a sign from somewhere."

They could still hear screeching birds and monkeys. Suddenly, as if on cue, they both heard a loud growl just on the inside of the jungle foliage. A large jaguar walked into the clearing and growled at them menacingly. Broad and thick, it roared twice and started to move toward them.

Jack whispered, "Don't run! He'll chase us! They kill by biting you on the back of the head and sinking their teeth into your brain!" Jack began to back up slowly, raising his arms and growling menacing, trying to look large and ferocious! The jaguar advanced slowly, growling and staring at Jack.

Zenadia stood where she was. She turned and looked at Jack as he was backing up, now waving his arms and growling loudly. She started to giggle at Jack.

Jack saw her out of the corner of his eye. Zenadia wasn't moving and now she was laughing out loud at him, holding her stomach with her arm and almost doubling over. He stopped and looked at her.

Zenadia, still chuckling, turned back to the jaguar and made noises like a series of small chirps, two growls and one sharp bark. The jaguar stopped advancing toward Jack, and trotted over to Zenadia, nuzzling against her legs. Jack put his hands on his hips and rolled his eyes. "What the hell?" he said.

Zenadia rubbed the big cat's thick fur and was apparently still talking to him with a series of chirps, growls and making a clucking sound with her throat.

Jack, still in disbelief, said to Zenadia, "Did you make a new friend, or do already know him?"

Zenadia, kept up her conversation with the big cat. "His name is Royal, and he wants to help us! He's going to show us an easier route through the jungle. He is worried you won't make it." She smiled broadly, "He wants to know why you were waving your arms around like that. He said it made you look silly!" She started to laugh again, and to Jack's amazement, it looked and sounded like the jaguar was laughing too!

Jack smiled, even though the joke was being made at his expense. "Really? Did he say anything else?"

Zenadia said, "He says your jaguar accent is pretty shitty! You should stick to human speak!"

"Ha, ha, very funny! OK, no hard feelings then." He started to reach out to pet the big jaguar, but Royal roared at him and Jack yanked back his hand. "What's wrong?" he asked.

Zenadia laughed again. The jaguar chirped at her. "He said he was just kidding! You can pet him!"

"Uh, that's OK," he smiled at the jaguar. "Let's just get to the gold mine!"

Royal ran into the thick jungle followed by Zenadia and Jack.

The PT boat had been charging upstream for hours on the deeper channel. Once they got to the cross stream, they turned left and headed on what was now the downstream leg of the river tributary that had become too shallow to let them follow the boat with the kidnapped girls. Bill knew from the maps he had, that this river would lead them to where the gold mine was and, hopefully, the girls. The only rub would be if the soldiers had found the gold and went back downstream to the main river. Bill had talked this over with Charlie, Manolo, Kimmi, John and Miguel. They all believed it would not be simple to just waltz in, grab the gold and run away with it. It had been lost for decades and whoever was hiding it, would not give it up easily. So, they all hoped they had time to get back there, engage the enemy and free the girls.

Bill was at the helm, Charlie and John were on the twin machine guns, Manolo and Kimmi were on the Oerlikon cannon.

Miguel was lying flat on his stomach on the bow searching the dark water for anything that they might crash into. Because the river here was narrow and was a deep brownish green color, they had to cut their speed down considerably. Bill was thinking about the gold bar in his pocket. That could be the talisman that would earn them the favor of the tribe and help them rescue the girls.

Suddenly, Charlie, as if reading his thoughts said, "Hey Bill, do you think those natives, if there are any, will be friendly or will try to kill us?"

Bill looked over at her and said, "I hope to bring them their treasure back and earn their trust that way. It is only one small brick of gold, but it seems to have magic powers over people. Maybe they cannot be whole until every brick is in its right place. Who knows?" He shrugged and called up to Miguel on the bow, "Is the speed OK Miguel?"

"*Si, Capitain,*" he called back. "I can see ahead, but the water is too dark. At least there are no floating logs like on the Amazon River!"

Bill nodded. He steered a straight course down this tributary river which was getting wider as it approached the Atrato River. He believed at their current speed they would reach the gold mine in less than two hours. He prayed they would be in time.

CHAPTER TEN

THE FIGHT TO THE DEATH FOR FREEDOM

THE THREE GIRLS ON THE KIDNAPPER'S BOAT, Gwendolyn, Cazzy and Jackie, were still lying on the deck in the stern of the boat. Because of the heat, they were not being forced to lay under the heavy blanket, but were still exposed to the sun. They lay on their sides talking in short whispers, as there were still two soldiers onboard with them, but on the bridge several feet away. "What do you think they did with Jazmine?" asked Jackie. She was frightened and was afraid for all of their lives.

Cazzy said, "They probably wanted her for some kind of trump card, just in case they had trouble with anyone trying to rescue us. But without the people on the PT boat, we are pretty helpless out here! Who the hell is left to help us?"

Gwendolyn whispered, "I heard them talking. I don't think they know that we speak Spanish, even though the dialect is different. It is like you said Cazzy. The men all want to use us, but the Generals won't let them. But there is no rescue or ransom for us. Once we get to Cartagena, they are selling us for as much money as they can get." She paused, "I just want to go home…" she started to cry again, but stopped because one of the soldiers had started to walk back to check on them. The girls were silent as he walked around them. They didn't dare look at him, only down at the deck and at each other. He returned to the bridge and spoke briefly to his comrade. They both scanned the jungle with binoculars, looking for potential threats.

The girls continued. Jackie said, "I can't believe *Señor Roberto* was in on this! I feel so betrayed! Like he just wanted to use us! He left us in the hands of these evil men and now our lives are ruined!" She shook her head, fighting back the tears.

Cazzy, the tough one said, "You both need to put on your big girl panties right now! We may need to fight our way out of this! I don't know how, or when or where, but I'll be damned if I'm going to let some smelly soldier, or a sheikh, or a millionaire playboy touch this body! Oh, hell no!" The other two nodded in agreement and laughed silently at her brashness. None of them were big, tough, or trained to fight, but this was life and death. Cazzy continued, "Even a rabbit will turn and fight the fox when he is cornered. That's what we need to do. For now, keep your ears and eyes open and be ready for anything!" Gwendolyn and Jackie both nodded and all three said prayers that they would be tough and ready when the time came.

General de Luna, Supreme General Velasco and the four soldiers, all carrying heavy bags of gold, struggled back up the path to the jungle. Two soldiers were up front and two were in the back. Between them was Jazmine and the two generals. They did not know they were being followed. The tribal chief Jojo and his wife Sulu, had an interest in seeing that the kidnapped girls were rescued, even if they and their tribe had to do it themselves. They had observed the men taking their gold and saw Jazmine sitting off to one side. It was interesting that they observed she was looking around as if trying to plan her escape. Most young girls would be frightened, but she seemed as though she was waiting for an opportunity. They thought maybe the other girls they had heard of from the shaman, were just as tough and didn't need any help. To get their gold back was a simple matter. They could kill these infidels with little trouble. They were nothing. But the bigger prize was getting the one missing brick back that would make their tribe whole again. They had to wait and plan carefully for that.

It took them over an hour to get the bricks back to the entrance to the jungle. At that point they were all sweating profusely. Tired and thirsty, they stopped for a drink from their canteens. General de Luna politely offered his canteen to Jazmine, but she shook her head quietly, refusing to drink after this dirty sweaty soldier, who wanted to take her life away from her.

Jazmine sensed her father was somewhere near her. She didn't know how or why, but she felt her dad's presence. She did not feel as if the PT boat was close, so she wondered how the heck her dad would have gotten near her. Her rational mind told her she was just imagining things, but her heart and her instincts told her something different. *The only way he could get here without the PT boat was over the jungle, and that would be suicide,* she thought. She was determined to keep her eyes and ears open. If her dad was here, then he would need help to get her and her friends away, and she was itching for the chance to deal with these bastards.

****

Bill, on the PT boat sensed they were getting close. In spite of the mists, heavy jungle and the high canopy of the trees, his dead reckoning skills told him the high peak of the gold mine would appear any minute. "Look sharp everybody!" he said, "We are getting really close!" He continued to scan the jungle and took out his binoculars, looking above the trees, hoping the mists would part long enough so that he could make out the tall spire of the mountain.

Suddenly he saw it. The mists had parted just long enough to see the conical shape of the mountain peak. Charlie, on the forward gun turret on the starboard side, saw it too. "Bill," she said excitedly, "there it is!"

"All stop!" Bill said quietly, as he pulled back on the throttle of the PT boat. He put the boat into its muffled formation to dampen the sound, lest they be heard by the enemy. He said to everybody, "Battle Stations," but did not throw the lever that would sound the alarm. Charlie and John on the twin machine guns, with Manolo and Kimmi on the Oerlikon cannon, all racked their guns into firing positions and removed the safeties. Miguel scrambled off the bow and jumped into the bridge, ready to take over the helm for Bill if he had to.

Bill moved the heavy boat forward slowly and quietly in stealth mode. He whispered to Charlie, "Can you switch places with Miguel and bring up your sharp shooter rifle, please? The girls may still be aboard. If we can take out whoever is on the boat, we might be able to grab the girls and make a run for it. If we can avoid putting us all in harm's way by avoiding a firefight, so much the better!" Charlie nodded and jumped out of the gun turret. She raced into the charthouse and descended the ladder. She grabbed her high powered sniper rifle, plus several extra clips of ammo. She ran up the ladder and stood next to Bill at the helm. "Where do you want me?" she asked.

Bill said, "Next to me here in the bridge, behind the Kevlar shield. We can't use heavy firepower, but they can! If we can get into position, then you need to shoot to kill. No prisoners!" he added.

Charlie took aim forward, preparing herself. "You didn't need to tell me that. Did you think I was going to send them a box of candy?"

Bill laughed in spite of the tension. "No, I reckon not!" He looked over at Miguel, who had taken Charlie's place at the starboard twin machine gun. "Are you locked and loaded, Miguel?"

"Si, Capitain!"

He looked back at John on the port gun and also Manolo and Kimmi on the cannon. "Are you all ready?" he called out quietly. They nodded in affirmation.

"OK," said Bill, "No wild shooting! Be careful. Let's get our girls back!" They moved out slowly and carefully.

The two soldiers guarding the girls on the General's boat were getting tired of waiting. They had been left here to watch these teenagers and felt they were being left out of the action. Both were only 20 years old and had been looking at the girls with lust ever since they had been brought aboard. The first one named Esteban, said to his partner, Ricco, "Tired of waiting around, Ricco! They won't be back for an hour or more. Let's take a turn at these *putahs*!" he said.

Ricco, the more cautious one said, "Better not Esteban! The General said he would feed us to the fish if we molested them!"

"Ha! Who's going to know? The others are in the cave somewhere and our brothers are in the jungle! Now is the perfect time!" He could already feel himself getting excited. "I'm going after the Puerto Rican. She makes me hot!"

"You can go. Not me! I'll keep a lookout for you, though!"

Esteban started back towards the girls who were still lying on the deck. Jackie, his intended target, was lying between Cazzy and Gwendolyn. The girls saw him coming back, but didn't dare move. He stepped between them and, grabbing Jackie around the waist, pulled her up. She started to scream, and he clamped his hand over her mouth. With his other hand he tried to feel her breasts, but she fought him off with her arms and hands, instinctively protecting her front. He began kissing her neck as she fought against him. Ricco, still at the helm had forgotten that he was supposed to be on lookout. He had turned around to watch Esteban and the pretty dark haired girl struggle. In spite of himself, he began to move back towards them, hoping to take his turn with one of the other girls. He was halfway back to them when the PT boat rounded a bend in the river.

That's when all hell broke loose.

Bill, driving the boat saw them first. Immediately, he knew what was happening. He shoved the throttle forward and the boat surged forward with a mighty roar! "Charlie," he screamed, "can that bastard!" But Charlie couldn't get a clear shot.

"I can't!" she yelled at Bill, "I might hit the girl!"

It was then that Cazzy, still lying on her side, heard the roar of the PT boat, reached out with her foot and kicked the soldier holding Jackie savagely on the side of his knee. He let out a scream and loosened his grip while he grabbed his knee in pain. At the same time, Jackie shot an elbow back into his stomach and he screamed again, doubling over in pain. Both Gwendolyn and Cazzy leaped to their feet and pulled Jackie down and away from him, back onto the deck. Esteban was left exposed and Ricco, who had stopped on deck when he heard the PT boat, turned around to see what was making the noise.

"Now Charlie! Now!" Bill screamed.

Charlie didn't hesitate. She fired two rounds, which hit them both in the chest and caused both soldiers to fly backwards off of the deck of the boat into the water, killing them instantly. Bill covered the distance between the two boats in less than five seconds, reversing the engines to stop their momentum going forward. As they pulled up next to the enemy boat, all three girls jumped onboard the stern of the PT boat, helped by Manolo and Kimmiko, who had leapt from their weapon to help them aboard. Kimmi shoved them through the day cabin and onto the bridge. Bill pushed them down and told them to stay there, behind the Kevlar protection. Manolo had returned to the Oerlikon cannon, while Kimmi stayed on the bridge to help with the girls. Bill drove them away from the enemy boat downstream. He turned the PT boat around and now facing the enemy boat, waited.

The three girls were crying and thanking Bill for saving them. They wanted to hug him, but Bill made them stay down.

"We still have to get Jazmine, her dad Jack and Zenadia back on board before we can celebrate!" he whispered to them. "We are still in a desperate situation! Please stay down and save your thanks for later!" The girls all nodded. "By the way," Charlie said leaning down to pat the girls on their backs, "nice work back there! I couldn't have gotten off a clear shot until you kicked the shit out of that guy!" The girls all laughed out of relief and desperation, now that they felt safe-at least for the moment.

On the shore, the six soldiers in the jungle heard the roar of the PT boat and also the two rifle shots. Four of them ran for their own boat, and climbed aboard, as the other two stayed back momentarily. As a group, they turned around and saw the PT boat watching them two hundred yards away. They had to wait for orders to attack. With dismay, they realized the three girls were missing. Also, their two comrades were now floating face down in the water, obviously dead. They were both angry and afraid at the same time. As professional soldiers, they knew their job was to attack, but they were sitting ducks here if the PT boat should open fire!

Next to the cave, the generals, Jazmine and the four soldiers also heard the PT boat and the two rifle shots. Supreme General Vasquez gave immediate orders. He and General de Luna would return to their boat and attack the PT boat. Two soldiers were to follow with as much of the gold as they could carry. The other two would bring the girl, Jazmine, back to the boat to use as a hostage. If they had to attack the PT boat before the soldiers could get there, then they were to wait in the jungle until the generals returned. All agreed and the two generals took off for their boat running as fast as they could.

Jack, Zenadia and their escort, Royal, the jaguar, came to the edge of the jungle and could see Jazmine and the four soldiers starting to make their way to the boat. Two of them held Jazmine between them so she couldn't run, while the other two struggled with as much gold as they could carry. Jack was about to run to his daughter's rescue, but Zenadia held him back. "I've got to save my daughter!" he whispered frantically to Zenadia.

She shook her head and held up her finger to her lips. "They aren't going anywhere," she said. Royal growled and made sounds with his throat. Zenadia said, "Royal says the natives are watching us. He says the jungle has eyes!"

That sent a shiver up Jack's spine. He nodded. "What's the plan then?"

Zenadia smiled. "A little diversion. Just be ready to attack, but do it quietly! No guns, because it will scare the natives and they might attack you! Wait for my signal and then go straight for Jazmine!"

"Wait, how will I know…?" But she was gone. Disappearing into the jungle, leaving Jack with Royal, who he still didn't trust. He looked over at the big cat, who smiled at him, then he was gone too, leaving Jack alone, watching his daughter and the four guards move away from him.

Jojo and Sulu, in spite of their ages were extremely agile. Flanked by 12 natives, they watched the same thing Jack was watching but 200 feet away. Unlike Jack, they blended into the jungle, which was why they had never been discovered. Known as the Ghost Tribe, they had only once been spotted by the outside world and any potential trespassers had met with a quick death and had become ghosts themselves!

Suddenly, Royal came and stood next to Jojo, who stroked his fur. Sulu put her arms around the big cat and whispered into his ear, while kissing him on the cheek. Royal made some clucking sounds to Jojo, who nodded. He whispered back to his tribesmen, who gathered around him. "Royal says the white man is going to attack the two soldiers who are holding his daughter. Z, the witch is here and will make a diversion. The two guards at the back are carrying our treasure. Take care of those two and take the gold back where it belongs. Do not let them see you!" The natives nodded and got into position.

Jack waited in silence. The two soldiers that held Jazmine were in front and the two that were lugging the packs of what looked like gold were behind. They were desperately trying to balance two heavy back packs and also two bags, which they drug behind them. *Look!* Thought Jack, *Gold bars were actually falling out of the bags due to the weight, and onto the jungle floor! These men would never make it back, but if he attacked the ones holding his daughter, the others would attack him, and it would all be for nothing!* He decided to wait a few seconds. He set down his AK-47 rifle and took out his metal telescoping nunchakus. He was an expert martial artist, and the nunchakus could generate up to 1,600 pounds of force, which would kill or seriously maim an enemy instantly. Zenadia said to use stealth, which meant no guns. It really didn't matter. Jack was angry enough to use his bare hands to kill these bastards who wanted to hurt his little girl and the others as well!

He didn't have to wait long. Just as the soldiers started to leave the clearing, Zenadia appeared in front of them. She was wearing war paint on her face, which made her look like a demon, a short, tight wrap-around skirt and nothing else. The soldiers gasped, as much as looking at her with fear, but also outright lust.

Suddenly the natives let loose a volley of blowgun darts, tipped in poison, hitting the last two soldiers who carried the gold on their backs. The men dropped instantly, both dead from the poison. Jack leapt into the clearing, yelling at the two remaining soldiers. They turned around, stunned, as they were still thinking about Zenadia who stood before them. Jazmine also turned around and started to yell to her dad to be careful. One guard was holding Jazmine, while the other was struggling to bring his rifle up to shoot Jack. Jazmine, using her skills as a martial artist, brought her hands up and over the soldier's forearm and pushed down hard. The move forced him to release her. She then snapped off a side kick which caught the other guard holding the gun in the side of his ribs. The force of her kick knocked him to the ground, where he had momentarily dropped his weapon. Jack pounced on the guard who had been holding Jazmine. He knocked the AK-47 rifle out of the guard's hands and swung his nunchakus at his head. The soldier ducked and produced a long, lethal looking combat knife. Jack shoved Jazmine out of the way, landing at Zenadia's feet. Zenadia quickly covered Jazmine for protection.

The guard who Jazmine had kicked was struggling to his feet. He picked up his gun and was leveling it at Jack, waiting for a clear shot. Zenadia held up her hand, holding her palm facing the soldier. Suddenly, his throat closed and he gasped for air. He dropped his weapon and brought both of his hands to his throat, trying to breathe. Zenadia brought her hand up above her head, causing the soldier to impossibly levitate in the air. Holding him there, she then flicked her wrist. The soldier was flung through the air as if he was a rag doll and crashed into the trees at the feet of the tribesmen. This was not lost on the Natives, as Chief Jojo whispered to Royal the jaguar, who ran to the vanquished guard and stood over him growling. At that instant, the guard woke up, his breathing restored only to see he was pinned down by a fierce jaguar. He managed one scream as Royal attacked him, then was silent after that.

Jack and the remaining guard circled each other. The natives would not interfere, and neither would Zenadia. Jazmine was about to jump up and help her dad, but Zenadia whispered to her that he didn't need their help.

It was true. Jack with his pent-up father's rage, but also the disciplined mind of a martial artist, began his attack. The soldier held out his knife, which looked like a military Ka-Bar. Jack held out his nunchakus straight at the soldier, spreading them out to the sides. Suddenly, he began running them through their motion, up and down, back and forth. Then over and under both his shoulders, with a whipping motion. The air whistled with the sound of the lightning-fast nunchakus. Finally, he stopped with his right hand over his right shoulder and his left hand under his right shoulder, each hand held one end of the "sticks." They circled, each looking for an opening. Jack's nunchakus were metal, each piece would telescope to its farthest position and were held together by a metal chain. The soldier would feint a jab move at Jack with his knife, trying to get Jack to commit, but each time Jack jumped back and then forward again, so as not to lose ground. As Bruce Lee had taught, Jack had his right foot forward and also his right hand forward, as they were his dominant side. Traditional boxers usually held their strong hand back, with their nondominant hand forward using smaller punches, keeping their dominant fist ready to deliver the lethal blow.

Suddenly, Jack stepped back and ran his nunchakus again, over and over, back and forth, as though to confuse the soldier. Moving the metal handles from his right hand to his left hand, then around his body, ending up with the one handle under his right armpit and the other in his right hand. Jack faked forward with his right hand, but the other handle remained under his armpit. He did that twice. The soldier with a yell charged at Jack, trying to stab his knife into him. Jack, instead of coming over the top with the nunchakus, grabbed the handle in his armpit with his left hand, and swinging up, knocked the knife out of the soldier's hand. He then passed the nunchakus into his right hand and hit the soldier across his head, knocking him to the ground. The blow wasn't lethal, but it dropped him to his knees and he fell forward with a loud thud, unconscious.

With a cry, Jazmine jumped free of Zenadia and ran over to her father and embraced him. They both hugged and started to cry, but Zenadia, who had put her top back on, came over and said, "It's not over Jack! There are still the three other girls, and we don't know the status of our people on the PT boat!"

Jack nodded. He looked back and saw some scary looking natives, tiny men in fierce war paint gathering up the gold. He also saw the jaguar, Royal standing over the body of the soldier he had attacked. He looked at Zenadia and Jazmine. "Let's get moving!" he said.

Both General de Luna and Supreme General Velasco raced toward their boat. At the same time, they saw two of the soldiers they had dispatched into the jungle to cover their back and their flank, also running toward the boat. They could see their four soldiers from the jungle were now on the boat, but the two original soldiers who had been left on the boat were either dead or had deserted. The girls were gone, too and it was likely they had been rescued by the crew of the PT boat.

Supreme General Velasco was running to the right and slightly behind General de Luna. They were still a hundred meters from their boat, when Supreme General Velasco was hit by a dart, shot out by one of the natives. With a scream he went down, grabbing his right calf and rolling on his back. Fortunately for him, it had not been tipped in poison, but hurt, nonetheless. General de Luna stopped and tried to help him, but Velasco yelled at him to get the boat away from the mine and attack the Americans because he would be okay. General de Luna ran to the boat and, shouting orders, told his men to cast off. They drove the boat away from the beach two hundred meters in the opposite direction and then turned to face the PT boat.

Bill, John, Kimmi, Charlie, Manolo and Miguel saw the boat pull away from the shore. They had seen the six soldiers and the one general jump on the boat. There was no sign of Jack, Zenadia or Jazmine, but they hoped they were OK. Now there was no time to worry about their friends, as they knew they were about to be attacked. Fortunately, the three girls were now safely below deck, wrapped in bullet proof vests, which would protect them unless they were attacked by stinger missiles or hand grenades. John was sitting with them and attending to their needs, and especially reassuring them that they were now safe.

Bill gave orders quickly. They had not secured from Battle Stations, but to now be formal, Bill hit the button and the familiar sounds of Battle Stations rang out. They had changed places, as now Manolo was on the port machine gun, Charlie was on the starboard machine gun and Miguel was on the Oerlikon cannon. Kimmi went below to help her dad with the still shaken girls. Everyone was wearing helmets and life jackets. For the moment, the boats faced each other approximately 800 yards apart, both idling.

General de Luna was now realizing his worst fears. He had warned the Supreme General to just take the girls downriver, sell them and be done with it! Now the gold was gone, the girls were gone, Supreme General Velasco was hurt, several of their men were dead and there would be more to follow if they didn't blow this damn PT boat and its crew out of the water! He would not be handcuffed by the fact the girls were aboard. He and his men would shoot to kill and ultimately to destroy them all. He was secure in the knowledge that the blonde girl, Jazmine was back onshore with his four soldiers. They would kill these *gringos*, rescue the supreme general, and pick up his men and the girl. They could sell her for at least 500,000 or more, cut their losses and continue their trade tomorrow. But first, they had to get past this PT boat! He directed his shooters to man the two machine guns on the sides of the boat and the rest to lie flat with their AK-47 machine guns, two in front and two on the sides. They would begin their approach immediately!

Like jousters in ancient Camelot, the two boats began roaring forward heading straight toward each other! Bill yelled out to his crew, "Bring your weapons to bear in front! Lock and load! Miguel, when we pass them, release a full volley from the stern!" Bill crossed himself twice, "May God be with us!" he yelled to no one in particular.

The PT boat was doing 35 knots and the enemy boat was doing 30 knots and closing very fast.

General de Luna yelled, "Open fire, now!" The soldiers let loose a volley of automatic fire.

Bill yelled out, "Commence firing! Fire at will! Commence firing! Fire at will!" Charlie and Manolo opened up, concentrating their fire on the approaching vessel. The waves on the river had been whipped up by the motions of the boats and many of the shots went high and wide. Neither Captain Bill or General de Luna would change their heading and were still heading straight for each other! Charlie, alarmed, yelled at Bill, "Hey Bill, there is no second place for a game of chicken!"

With a maniacal laugh, Bill shoved the throttle all the way forward. "Increasing to flank speed, Charlie! What do you think of this little adventure now?!" he screamed over the roar of the engines. Charlie resumed firing, as they were almost on top of the approaching boat!

At the last second, Bill juked his wheel to the left, to protect the young girls, he reasoned, which caused the enemy boat to pass on his right side and directly into Charlie's line of fire. She did not waste a moment, as her twin machine guns, firing 1400 rounds per minute found their mark and ripped up the side of the General's vessel. As the boat passed, Miguel on the Oerlikon cannon opened fire, ripping part of their transom out.

General de Luna's men would not be denied, as they returned fire from their own stern at the PT boat. Both boats, turned again to return to the joust! This time, because of the tight turning arc, Bill had to bring his port side to bear, as Manolo opened fire on the enemy boat, finding its mark. Suddenly Manolo had to duck down as the line of fire shot over him and tore apart the day cabin, and almost killed Bill on the bridge, as he dove out of the way. Charlie, screamed in spite of herself as she ducked down in the gun turret, which was lined with Kevlar. After the boats had passed, Miguel returned fire with the Oerlikon cannon. Both Charlie and Manolo spun their machine guns around, following the boat with tracer fire.

The smoke began billowing from the enemy boat, as Charlie, Manolo and Miguel had all struck their intended targets. Several of the general's men were either dead or dying. Fortunately, no one on the PT boat had been hit, but the boat itself, had sustained damage. They could hear the girls below deck screaming, as several bullets had passed through, but they were all okay. They were still traveling in the opposite direction. Bill turned and slowly moved toward the enemy boat, which had stopped dead in the water and was apparently sinking.

Over his megaphone, Bill yelled, "Come about and surrender your boat!"

"Go to hell!" came the reply in Spanish.

"Rack your weapons!" yelled Bill to his crew.

Suddenly, General de Luna and one of his soldiers, apparently, the only survivor, both opened fire on the PT boat. The soldier was on the port machine gun and de Luna held an AK-47 standing on the bow. Charlie, who was in a better position, fired on the gunner on the port machine gun, killing him with one short burst from the machine gun. Bill had retrieved his Winchester repeating rifle from the bridge and holding it above the glass windshield, took aim at the general and fired a shot directly through his heart! General de Luna, flipped over backwards and fell dead in the water, floating with his face down.

Bill throttled down and slowed the engines, letting his boat drift towards the shore. "Keep your eyes open!" he yelled to his crew. "There may be more of them!"

Supreme General Velasco had watched this unfold from the shadows of the edge of the jungle. He knew his options were diminishing, as General de Luna and many of his soldiers were dead. He still had hope that the four guards he had left behind to bring out the girl, and the gold were still alive and would help him salvage something out of this mess. He saw the PT boat make it to shore. Just as he hoped, no one had missed him. He saw the crew of the PT boat disembark and walk down the gangplank, which had been placed there by one of the young men on the boat. He saw the man known as Bill, who was the captain walk down to the sand. He was followed by a tall, blond woman about his age. Then came another older man, a young pretty girl and the two dark complected young men. There was no sign of the three young girls, but they had to be aboard. They stood on the sand looking into the jungle, as if waiting for someone or something. They did not have to wait long.

Suddenly, he saw the girl they had captured, Jazmine striding down past him toward the group. She was followed by a man, who may have been her father. He glanced up the path and saw a young woman, who had the face of a demon painted on her, striding boldly toward him. Somehow, she radiated danger and he made a quick decision. Raising his AK-47 high above his head, as the demon girl walked by, he brought the butt of his gun directly down on her head. She screamed and grabbed the back of her head where she had been struck and fell face down in the sand. For reasons unknow to him, she turned her face toward him. Her eyes were colored red and blazed with fury. In a guttural tone, straight from the grave and meant only for him she said, "Satan is coming for you Velasco!" Then she passed out.

"Zenadia!" Charlie screamed and started to run toward her daughter. Supreme General Velasco, in spite of his sudden fear over what she said, stood over her body and fired a volley of machine gun fire over their heads.

"The next round will take all of you out!" he screamed at them in English. They were only about 30 feet away from him, but Jack and Jazmine were only a few feet away.

Bill, angry at himself, realized they had gotten off the boat without weapons. "What is it you want? All of your soldiers are dead. We have the girls. They are safe! There is no way out for you! Surrender now and we won't kill you!"

Velasco, threw back his head and laughed. Quickly he strode toward Jack and swung the butt of his rifle, hitting him under the chin. Jack flew backwards and fell on his back. He was dazed, but still conscious. Jazmine screamed and tried to get to her dad. Velasco reached out and grabbed her by her arm and shoved the barrel of the gun against her temple. "Stay where you are, or I will shoot you dead right now!" he screamed. Everybody froze. "I will tell you what I am going to do. I am going to take this girl onto your boat. I know that is where the other girls are. I'm going to take them downriver and sell them as planned. You people can sit here on this damn beach or swim home. I really don't care!

"This mission has been a cluster fuck from the get! Now I am going to get the hell away from you and there isn't a damn thing you can do about it! Now back off!" He yelled to the boat, "You girls get up on deck now! Or I will start shooting!"

After a minute, the three girls came up on deck and stood by the rail.

Velasco smiled. "Just as I thought! Now we will leave here and finish our little adventure together!"

Cazzy and Gwendolyn were looking at the general and the rest of the party. They had been rescued only to be captured again. Jackie was looking around.

She was the first to see him and the sight made her scream at the top of her lungs!

Behind the PT boat walking out of the water, was a man or something that resembled a man! He only had on the tattered remains of pants, no shirt, shoes or hat. He was covered in mud, slime and seaweed. Everyone turned around and looked at him. He stared straight at Supreme General Velasco and began to grin eerily at him.

He looked like a zombie! Death incarnate, here before them all! Velasco dropped to his knees. His rifle fell uselessly into the sand. He held out his hands in front of him as if in surrender. He began to cry. *"¡Diablo, diablo!"* he screamed. *"¡Satanás ha venido a matarme!* (Satan has come to kill me!). He tried to rise up as the creature ran at him screaming his name over and over.

"*¡Velasco!"* it screamed, "*¡Velasco! ¡Debes morir ahora!* (You must die now!)."

The girls were screaming. Everyone fell back in absolute fear. It was Gwendolyn who suddenly said, "It is *Señor Roberto!"*

Roberto fell savagely on Velasco hitting him over and over with his fists. He kicked him in the groin and then on his head. He punched him hard in the face, knocking out several teeth, as Supreme General Velasco tried to cover his face-the face of a true coward. Roberto dragged him to his feet and, with both arms, put a choke hold on the general, shutting off his air. Velasco struggled but Roberto rode him down all the way to the sand.

Bill thought he should stop this, but before he could move, with a mighty roar, Roberto twisted Velasco's neck with his elbow, causing it to break with a loud snap! Velasco shook violently for only a second in the throes of death and then was still. Roberto held him tightly by the neck, even though he was already dead. There was an eerie silence in the jungle, as though the thousands of birds, monkeys and other creatures had been watching this battle and all holding their breath. Suddenly, Roberto began to cry, the adrenaline rushing out of his body. Finally, Jack and Bill came over and helped him to release Velasco's body. They pulled him away. He sat sobbing on the beach. Jazmine was the first to reach him and she threw her arms around him. "I knew you wouldn't have betrayed us! I knew you wouldn't have betrayed us!" she said over and over again. Suddenly, Gwendolyn, Cazzy and

Jackie ran down the gangplank. Reaching Roberto and Jazmine, they all hugged him, crying. They had no idea how he got there or what he had been through, but they knew he had somehow gotten here to save them!

Charlie ran to Zenadia, who was starting to move. She held her, rocking her gently. Suddenly, without warning, Zenadia came awake and, with a roar, jumped to her feet. "What happened to me? How the hell did that guy," she looked over at the dead general, "knock me out? No one does that to me!" she yelled angrily.

Charlie smiled, "Maybe you're more human than you give yourself credit for!" She hugged Zenadia again. "No matter what, you are still my beautiful daughter and I love you!"

Zenadia smiled and said, "OK! Is he dead? If not, I want to kill him!"

Charlie hugged her tightly, "It's over," she said simply.

The situation was finally calming down. Jack, who was still a little dazed, asked the girls to step back and give *Roberto* some room to breathe. Jack asked him, "Can you stand up?"

Roberto nodded and slowly got to his feet. Everyone was staring at him. He smiled and waved. "Hi," he said weakly, "I am *Roberto*. I am the one who is responsible for all of this mess!"

Bill asked him point blank, "Were you a participant of their plan?"

Roberto shook his head. "No, but I was an *unwilling* part of *their* plan. They knew I brought students down here to teach English. Obviously, Velasco plotted his revenge against me for something I did many years ago, then decided to take the girls and sell them off as a little bonus." He looked around, "I don't know who you all are or why they stopped here, but it was fortunate for me, otherwise I never would have found you!"

Bill asked, "What did you do that would make them reach halfway around the world to get at you? Plus plan this whole military mission? By the way, the reason we landed here was because they got greedy. There is a vast amount of gold in that mine and they wanted to get it!"

Roberto smiled and took a deep breath. "Years ago, I kind of got addicted to gambling in high school. That General," he gestured toward Velasco's body, "was the cousin of a girl I was dating. She told me to stop gambling and stop seeing him, because she knew he was bad. I was a pretty good football player, but I wasn't getting any offers for college."

Bill smiled, "Uh, excuse me, but aren't you a little small to be a football player? With all due respect, of course!"

Roberto laughed weakly, as he was really wiped out. "Sorry, that's what we call it. It is known as soccer in the U.S."

They laughed, as Roberto continued. "So, they wanted me to throw the championship game and help me win gambling money to go to college. I agreed, but at the last second, I couldn't go through with it. I helped my team win the game and went on to play in college and some professional soccer. They were going to kill me, so my dad went to him and, according to Velasco, beat him within an inch of his life. He told him to leave me alone, and he did. But he never forgot.

"I have been back here many times, but why he chose this trip to attack, I don't know why. When the girls and I were done with our teaching, we went to a cantina to celebrate. That is the last thing I remember before he and his men threw me off a cliff and down into a waterfall."

Jack spoke up, "What? They threw you off a cliff? How the hell did you survive? And how did you get here?" he asked incredulously.

Roberto smiled, "All good questions. I guess I was unconscious for a while, but the cold water revived me. I missed hitting several large boulders by inches. The next thing I knew, I was being hurled down a river. Eventually, I wound up on the shore in the jungle. I felt broken and bruised, but there was no way out, so I fashioned a float out of driftwood and got back in the water. I figured it would dump me back downriver, where I might find a town or village. I knew I had no chance in the jungle. As long as there were no piranha or caiman, I thought I might be okay. Somehow, after a while, I hit some rapids upstream of here. It almost killed me. I floated again for a while. This morning I had almost given up, but I spotted the PT boat before the attack. I hoped it was the same one I had been told about by Jazmine. I thought, how many PT boats can there possibly be? So, I waited until the time was right. I wanted to see if Velasco was still behind this and confront him. Mostly I felt like I had to do something to help get the girls back. I felt responsible because I had not been able to protect them."

They were all silent for almost a minute.

Charlie spoke up. "Are we done then? Can we leave?"

Suddenly the jungle curtain parted and several of the most fierce looking natives they had ever seen entered the clearing. They were all less than five feet tall, but were scary, nonetheless. At their feet was a large jaguar, who was growling and roaring menacingly. Two older natives, one man and one woman holding long spears, stepped forward away from the rest of the tribe. Another man, dressed in more ceremonial garb, but without weapons stood to the side of them.

Zenadia moved forward and stood in front of them. She bowed to them and spoke rapidly to them in their native language. They spoke back to her.

"You are Jojo and Sulu," she said. *We honor your presence. Thank you for sending Royal to find us and bring us to you. We would have been lost without him!"*

They both smiled, *"You are the famous Z, whose legend lives in the jungle. You knew Royal was sent to find you and your friend as he blundered through our jungle. How did you ever manage, dragging him along?"* They all laughed, including Zenadia and Royal.

Zenadia asked, *"Are you going to allow us to give you back what had been stolen from you many years ago? Then will you allow us to leave in peace? No one needs to know of your existence. None of us will ever return here. They have all that they want, the kidnapped girls."*

Jojo looked at his wife Sulu. He whispered to her and also to the shaman next to her. Jojo looked at Zenadia and slowly nodded his head once.

Zenadia bowed low and stepped back. She walked over to Bill, who was standing next to Charlie. "Can you please bring it? You will have to hand it to them, because the curse is on you, and they will have to absolve you."

"I didn't steal it!" Bill said unhappy at this turn of events.

"No, but you accepted it from Maltilda. Why do you think he was so happy to give it to you in the first place?!"

Bill rolled his eyes, thinking, *Shit, how did I get myself into this?* "OK, let's do it!" He pulled out the gold brick from his pocket and walked with Zenadia to the Chief and his wife.

"Bow down!" Zenadia whispered fiercely. Bill did as he was told.

"Get on your knees and hold the brick out to them!"

Bill, quietly rolling his eyes, but so no one could see him, did it.

"Look down at the sand!" Zenadia whispered fiercely. "Don't look him in the eye! He is a chief!"

Bill looked down. He felt the Chief take it from his hand, but then he gasped, glancing up as the Chief raised his sword high above his head. He waited for the blow that would end his life.

Slowly, the Chief brought it down and touched both of Bill's shoulders lightly.

"Stand up and bow. The curse is lifted!" said Zenadia.

Bill straightened up. He bowed again, "Thank you." He started to reach out his hand to shake hands with the Chief, but Royal, the jaguar jumped between him and growled. Bill stepped back and said, "Uh, sorry! Never mind."

"He is royalty! You can't touch him!" hissed Zenadia sharply.

Bill nodded and bowing again, turned and returned to the boat, while Zenadia continued to talk to the natives. She was petting Royal and kissing him while he licked her face. After a few minutes she returned to the PT boat, while the tribe disappeared back into the jungle, carrying the final gold brick, which would make their tribe whole again.

They gathered around Zenadia. What was that all about?" asked Jack.

Zenadia smiled, "They were going to invite us to a

ceremony where they replaced the gold brick, which would restore their village."

"And?" asked Jack.

"I thanked them for the offer, but they are a secretive tribe and we need to forget we ever met or saw them. Zenadia looked around at everyone. "Does everyone understand that? We have to forget about this place forever."

Jazmine looked at her three friends, who all nodded at her. "I don't think any of us want to think about this place ever again!" she said, "Their secret is safe with us!"

Everybody cheered. Bill said, "Let's get everyone aboard and move back upriver. Maybe Manolo can make us a good lunch. I'm sure we are all starved." He looked at Roberto. "In fact, some maybe more than others! We'll have to backtrack to get back to the Artato River, because it is too shallow to go down river, which is so strange. Then we can be in Colon in two days. What do you say, girls? Ready to get back to the good old USA?"

The girls all cheered as everyone boarded the PT boat.

Bill smiled. "OK, I'm going to get on the radio to Jack's next-door neighbor with the ham radio and see if he wants to get Lisa and some of the other parents on the line to communicate with us. I am sure everyone is frantic to hear from you girls!"

The girls all nodded and started talking excitedly. They knew their parents would be sick with worry.

It was then that they heard the loud sounds of heavy military helicopters coming down through the canopy of the jungle. There were two Airbus helicopters AS532 Super Puma/Cougars dropping out of the sky with full Panamanian Army insignias. Technically, they were not an official army, but part of the Panama Defense Forces. They landed on the shore next to the PT boat. Several military soldiers got out and walked over to the PT boat, carrying automatic weapons. They did not point their rifles at them, but stood at the ready. No one on the boat dared to move.

Finally, an officer stepped down and walked over to the PT boat. He eyed Bill and decided he was in charge. The officer saluted him. In English he said, "Are you the captain of this vessel?"

Bill nodded warily, worried about this new wrinkle with the local military and what it could mean. He returned the salute, even though he didn't wear a uniform, or had an insignia reflecting his rank. The officer smiled.

I am Major Nando Archuletta, and I have been sent here by my Commanding Officer at the request of my daughter Claudia to find you! Is there a Jazmine here, who I may greet?"

Jazmine, standing on the stern deck waved and said, "I'm Jazmine sir!" She went over to the gangplank and walked across the sand to greet him. With a slight bow and a curtsey, she smiled up at him.

The Major saluted her. "My daughter, Claudia, who you were so kind to in Colon has sent us many kilometers to find you and rescue you. However," and he looked around, "it seems you have already been rescued and are completely safe! This I am very happy about, and I will tell Claudia that you are safe and she too will be very happy." He looked around again. The enemy boat was destroyed, but still floating mostly submerged in the water and there were many dead bodies, most of whom were wearing uniforms. His smiles turned to a frown.

"There seems to be many dead soldiers here, some of whom are wearing our own military uniforms." He looked up at Bill. "Sir, do you have an explanation? I may need to notify the next of kin of these men and I would like to know how and why they died."

It was *Señor Roberto* who spoke up. In Spanish he said, "Sir, my name is Roberto Morales. I am from Panama City and I was a soccer star from Panama City High School, many years ago."

Suddenly Major Archuletta stopped him. He pointed, "You! Roberto Morales! You are the one who won the game to beat Oxford! I was in the stands. I went to Panama City! I won a lot of money from my friends at Oxford for that game! You made that bicycle kick in the last second to win the game! I spilled my beer all over my girlfriend! She was so mad at me! That was a great kick!" He smiled. "So glad to meet you after all of these years!"

Roberto smiled back. "Thank you, but unfortunately, many others were not so pleased. Your own Supreme General Velasco has had a vendetta for me for many years, as I was supposed to throw that game for the benefit of him and his gambling friends, but could not."

"The Supreme General was in on this?" asked Major Archuletta incredulously.

Roberto nodded, "Yes and so was General de Luna. They were smuggling our girls to Cartagena to be sold to the highest bidders as slaves. Plus, they were running drugs, other women and smuggled gold for their own benefit." He looked down and shook his head as if to say it was very sad, but continued, "Sir, I do not know what these soldiers were doing here. Either following orders or following in the rape and pillage they were about to commit, but I do know that they tried to kill my friends and me, but were thwarted from their evil plans by these men and women."

Even before he was through speaking, Major Archuletta was nodding his head in agreement. "We have known there were some soldiers in our division doing these things, but we didn't know who or to what extent. You all," and he looked over at everyone, suddenly speaking English again, "have done us a great service here! No doubt you are anxious to go home and return to your families. How may we assist you in this matter?"

Bill spoke up, "Major, if you could get word to the Consulate that we have the girls and they are safe, that would be a help. I am going to communicate with their families now and we will sail up river, make the turn, and then sail back down river to the Atrato. Then we will sail to Colon where we will put them on a plane back to the United States."

Major Archuletta smiled and bowed his head. "That we will most certainly do!"

Jazmine spoke up, "Major, sir. Can you please tell Claudia thank you from the girls and me, and that we appreciate all you have done for us! We promise to return with lots of nice clothes for them to wear as soon as we can!"

The major smiled and bowed slightly to the pretty girl, who was so eager to return to the place where her life had nearly been placed in forfeit, just to be kind once again to people she barely knew. If everyone in the U.S. was like this, then, he thought, maybe having closer relations to the United States wasn't such a bad idea. "I will do that exactly, miss!" he said. He turned to his soldiers and in Spanish told them to load the bodies of the dead troops into the helicopter. They would take them back to the base and try to sort this all out. Somehow, he hoped to put a positive spin on the lives of the soldiers, who had been led astray by the two generals. For the two of them, they would be buried in disgrace as a warning to all who would stray from the nobility of military service for the country of Panama!

Finally, the troops boarded the two helicopters and, after a few seconds of spinning their blades, began to hover in the air. Then they took off with a thunderous noise, heading for Panama City.

Bill went into the charthouse on the PT boat. He began to use his radio to try to get through to Jack's next-door neighbor.

Lisa Paris had fallen asleep on the couch in her living room. It was almost 4:00 pm. She was exhausted, having slept in starts and stops since her husband Jack had left for Panama to find their daughter Jazmine and the rest of the girls. Her son, Tommy, stared at the TV, numb from worry about his dad and sister and unable to focus.

Suddenly there was a loud knock over and over again on their front door. Both Lisa and Tommy leapt to their feet, hearts racing and ran over to the door. Before they could say anything, the familiar voice of Mike, their next-door neighbor rang out. "Lisa, Lisa!"

Lisa threw open the door. Mike hugged her tight, "They are all safe! They are on the PT boat and are headed home!" I just spoke to Jack on the radio! He wants to talk to you!" Lisa started to cry and almost fainted.

They ran over to his house and into his garage where he

kept the ham radio. Mike keyed the microphone, "Jack. Come in Jack! Over!"

"I'm here Mike, did you get Lisa? Over"

Lisa said, "I'm here Jack. Are they all okay?"

"Yes. All of the girls are OK." Unexpected static kept the transmission from continuing. They listened to the high pitch noise for almost a minute.

"Jack," Lisa keyed the microphone, "Jack! Can you hear me?"

"Yes, but barely. Listen, just tell the parents the girls are all OK and we are going to Colon to fly back home. We will be there in two days. I'm coming with them so they will be safe. We will be flying with Charlie and Zenadia. They helped us out a lot! When we get out of this jungle, we will try to contact you again. By then we may have cell phone reception! You and Tommy OK? Over."

"Yes, Jack. Thank God for you and Bill. And the rest of you heroes on the boat! Thank you! Bless you!"

THE END

EPILOGUE

A TIME TO HEAL

JACK PARIS, CHARLIE, ZENADIA, ALONG WITH the girls, Jazmine, Cassie, Gwendolyn and Jackie were assembled on the tarmac of the airport in Colon, next to Charlie's Cessna Citation X. They had been processed through Customs and were cleared to take off on a direct flight to the United States. Earlier, on the PT boat, they had all said their thanks to Bill, John, Kimmi, Manolo and Miguel. There were many hugs and tears to go around. The truth be told, the girls were all traumatized as to be expected, but were doing their best to keep it together.

Miguel had found Gwendolyn sitting by herself at the galley table below decks crying softly. He sat down next to her and put his arms around her. As he rocked her gently, her sobs became tears as she hung on to him. Shaking, she became racked with tears, as she gave into her emotions. "I just want to see, my mom, my dad and my little brother, Jason. I want to see my dogs, Moose and Gabriel." She continued to cry softly. Miguel didn't say a word, but kept holding her and rocking her.

After 20 minutes, she calmed down and kissed him tenderly on his cheek. "Thank you, Miguel," she whispered quietly. "I thought I was going to die in this awful jungle." They continued to hold each other for several more minutes. She took a deep breath and relaxed. Finally, Miguel released her and said, "Gwendolyn, the bad people are dead. That is what happens to bad people-they die. We are good people and we will get you home to your families. No one will bother you again. If you ever decide to return here again, please rest assured we, especially me, will protect you and make sure your adventure is a happy, safe one. OK?"

Gwendolyn nodded and smiled. "Thank you, Miguel!" She put her arms around him and hugged him fiercely.

Jazmine and her dad, Jack were standing on the tarmac together. Gwendolyn stood next to Miguel, cherishing the comfort he had shown to her. Cazzy and Jackie were talking quietly to Manolo and Kimmiko about the possibility of coming back down here to continue the good will started by Jazmine, but with the protection of the PT boat and its crew. They all started laughing as Bill and John joined the conversation and began telling the girls their measurements for designer jeans and how much it would cost them for this "personal protection!"

Finally, Charlie and Zenadia told everyone it was time to leave. The parents of the girls had all been alerted and would be anxiously awaiting at Buchannan Fields Airport in Concord.

Señor Roberto, still in Colon, had hoped to travel home with them, but because of the treachery and the events that had transpired, he was asked to meet with the military and the Panamanian government, which he was not too happy to do. It was a call from Major Archuletta that smoothed things over. He reassured Roberto that he was not at fault, and was being hailed as a hero for braving the falls, the rivers and the jungle to help to rescue the girls, who had fallen in harm's way. However, it was explained to him that the government needed to tie up loose ends, especially since the military had become involved, and he was, essentially a "loose end." There were dead soldiers and two dead generals who had to be accounted for. He was the one who would bear witness to the affairs of these men, as best as he could.

He was told he would be released back to the United States in one week or less and that he could continue to have a dialogue with his students and new-found friends on the PT boat. As an aside, several of the military leaders had wanted to meet him on a personal basis, as he was still considered a national treasure because of his soccer accomplishments. Even though it was many years ago, the people of Panama had long memories and many wished to meet the hero of the games, including the military brass!

As the girls and Jack began to board Charlie's plane, Jack suddenly turned around and ran to where Bill, John, Manolo, Kimmi, and Miguel were standing. He hugged them all, and with tears forming at the corners of his eyes, he said, "Thank you all! My family and I are now restored because of you! Bless you!"

Bill, in spite of himself, began to tear up and said, "You better get on that plane Jack. I've already made plans to visit Charlie in the States and if you miss that plane, we'll make you swim to California!"

Jack smiled and grabbed the big man in a bear hug. "Thanks Bill! See ya around Danville, Bill Treese!" And with that he charged up the ramp to be with his daughter and the girls he had come down to the Darién Gap to rescue. The most dangerous jungle in the world!

www.ingramcontent.com/pod-product-compliance
Lightning Source LLC
Chambersburg PA
CBHW070024120726
47909CB00003B/1054